MOVING ON

KAREN TUCCI

TRUE HEART ROMANCE

There are people in my life who've impacted me deeply. I met Nancy in 2004 when I started attending my first church as a saved adult. She was a light in this dark world. Just like Miss Clancy in this story, who loved on Sarah, Nancy loved on everyone in the church. She supported me and encouraged me to write. She's since gone home to be with Jesus – no longer in pain. It's too bad I couldn't have published this before she left this Earth, but everything is in God's time.

I love you, Nancy!

Contents

Karen's Other Books:

Stand Alone Books:

When the Dust Settles: A Sweet Romance with a Navy SEAL

G & G Security Series (Coming 2025)

(The characters from When the Dust Settles cross-over in this series)

Operation: Heal my SEAL Book 1

Operation: Find my SEAL Book 2

Operation: Keep my SEAL Book 3

Operation: Train my SEAL Book 4

Second Chance Series:

Starting Over

Moving On

Big L' Ranch Series

The Perfect Kiss: Book 1

The Perfect: Cowboy Book 2

The Perfect Match Book 3

The Perfect Christmas (Holiday Novella)

<u>The Perfect Sheriff Book 5</u>

Best Friends Series

<u>Let Me Carry You</u>

<u>Let Me Marry You</u>

YA Cumberland Christian Prep School Series

The Big Score (Coming 2025)

1

Sarah - Florida

Sarah Morris wiped a single tear that escaped the corner of her eye — a mere warning of the flash flood waiting to break the levies known as her eyelids. "I now pronounce you husband and wife. You may kiss your bride." The small, intimate crowd sounded like a packed stadium of rowdy Buccaneer fans as they erupted with hoots and hollers for the newlyweds.

Happiness washed over Sarah for the first time in years as she watched her daughter, Lily, kiss her new husband, Kurt. In fact, it was the first time she could recall authentically smiling since she'd left her dad's house in Maine. Truth be told, she didn't just *leave;* she ran. Since then, she'd pasted on a smile and kept trudging through life.

"I love you, Mom." Lily stopped at the first row of pews as she and Kurt held hands and headed down the aisle, ready to start their lives together.

When Lily and Kurt had met in high school, they were inseparable — attending each other's games when they weren't at their own, going to prom and the senior ball. Every free moment from athletics, they could have been caught snuggling on the couch studying for a test, watching a movie, or zonked out from either of the activities above. His gentleness with Lily impressed Sarah. She'd seen Kurt on the field and court. He could lose his cool, but she'd never seen him do that with Lily. He treated her with love and respect. Sarah was happy for both of them. She wouldn't want her daughter with anyone else.

Watching them grow together reminded her of her high school years with Lily's dad, Jake. She lost him in a car accident years ago. Had that never happened, Lily wouldn't have met Kurt. Sarah wouldn't have met Brandon either. *Focus, Sarah. Don't think about him today!*

"I love you too, Baby Girl." Sarah squeezed her daughter's hand briefly as Lily, Kurt, and their bridal party paraded out the door.

Call it a mid-life crisis, call it stupidity, call it anything you want; Sarah knew her misery – entirely self-inflicted – was to blame for her dismal mood. Instead of celebrating her fifth anniversary in a few months, she'd be doing the *same* old thing she'd been doing since she moved back to the *same* gated community in Florida where she once lived with Jake, her deceased husband, and Lily — nothing. She did nothing but take care of her basic daily living needs and teach online since she couldn't return to brick and mortar.

Her dad, Gus, and his fiancé, Barbara, arrived a week ago for the wedding. Sarah had forgotten how much she enjoyed talking with her dad around the table. Just when Sarah's life started to fall apart, Gus put his life on the path to happiness.

Barbara had been her dad's doctor. After his heart attack, she took responsibility for his in-home care. He found a new doctor so he could date Barbara. Eventually, they admitted they were in love but weren't in any rush to get married. Then they realized time wasn't on either of their sides, so now they are planning to marry but wanted Lily to have her day first.

Catching her dad's watchful eye, she forced a smile, feeling suffocated inside these four walls. Little bumps pricked at her arms. *What had she done? How could she have ruined her life so badly?* Sarah wasn't a *woe-is-me* kind of person, but that person slowly crept in like a thief in the night, stealing her joy over the past five years. Sarah stumbled through. Every. Single. Day. She pondered what her life would have been like if she hadn't walked away from Brandon.

"Come on, dear, let's meet the kids." Gus gently guided Sarah's elbow toward the aisle, ripping her from her thoughts. Though Gus never missed an opportunity to let Sarah know what Brandon was up to, he always seemed to understand what she was thinking and what she needed, even before she did.

When she announced that she couldn't stay in Maine any longer, Gus helped her pack without getting her to change her mind. She knew he wanted her to stay but loved her enough to let her go again. He tried to persuade Sarah to speak with Brandon before she left, but she couldn't. No one knew, but she started a letter to him before she left. Though she couldn't find it, the beginning was etched into her heart.

Brandon - I'm writing to let you know I'm in love with you! However, I have just as strong a feeling that we shouldn't get married now. Maybe someday, God willing.

She had lost the letter sometime during the move, which was probably for the best. What good would it do to tell Brandon she loved him if she couldn't marry him?

Once Lily and Kurt had graduated from high school, the three traveled to Florida. Sarah went to her familiar neighborhood, and the kids went to their dormitory at the University of Florida at Gainesville.

Through the years, she felt guilty about how things ended, but whenever she thought of contacting Brandon, she convinced herself he wouldn't want to hear from her, so she continued to wallow in her agony. The proverbial hole in Sarah's heart continued to grow even more gigantic.

"That was a beautiful wedding, wasn't it, dear?" Barbara asked, walking through the door Gus held open for the ladies.

"Yes, it was," Sarah replied automatically.

"How long until they leave for their next mission trip?" Gus inquired as they strolled to the table for the parents and grandparents adjacent to the head table.

"They leave in two days and won't return until the end of October." For some reason, this trip affected Sarah more than others. Maybe it was because it was the first time Lily didn't beg Sarah to go on, making it evident that Lily had matured.

The reception was beautiful with its pale blues and soft purples. When Sarah saw Lily in her halter-top sequined bridal dress dancing with Kurt, who complimented his wife's beauty with his rugged, handsome looks, she realized what an atrocious mental place she'd allowed herself to live in for years. Mist filled her eyes.

"Ladies and gentlemen..." the disc jockey's voice boomed through the speakers. "...let's give another round of applause for Mr. and Mrs. Kurt Anderson!

Kurt dipped Lily and kissed her as the clinking of glass rang throughout the reception. Sarah looked on in ambivalence. While she was happy for her daughter and Kurt, she couldn't help the melancholy twist in her gut that made her wish Brandon's arm was wrapped around her shoulder at this very moment.

Sarah caught Lily's aqua-green eyes two hours later as she and Kurt danced the night away. If there was one thing to be proud of in this life, it was how great Lily had turned out. Her bubbly spirit drew people to her, and her warm heart made it nearly impossible not to help others.

"Would you do me the honor of dancing with your old man?" Sarah turned to see her dad standing, palm up with his arm extended toward her.

The idea of dancing didn't sound horrible, but Sarah wasn't interested either. But when her dad flashed his charming smile, she couldn't let him down. "It would be *my* honor."

The song played on as Sarah and Gus reached the dance floor. "You deserve to be happy, sweetheart."

"We'll have to agree to disagree, " Sarah said, meeting Gus's eyes. "You've been telling me how badly I hurt him, so you can't tell me now that I have any right to be happy."

Gus shook his head. "I never realized how stubborn you are. You're just like your mother."

He led his daughter to another spot on the dance floor. "You've never been good at going easy on yourself, Sarah. Yes, Brandon's been just as miserable as you the past five years, but that doesn't mean you don't deserve to be happy. The way I see it, you have two choices. One, move on and find someone or something that makes you truly happy, or two, swallow your pride and try to fix things between you and Brandon."

"Second chances don't work. There's a reason it didn't work the first time. Isn't that what you always told me?"

"Perhaps I was wrong," Gus said, humble as usual. "Do your students get it right the first time, or do they have to regroup and try different strategies?"

Sarah refused to answer her dad. Whenever he started a conversation this way, she knew she didn't stand a chance, so she just agreed with him. "I get it. I need to figure out whether I want to move on or pursue Brandon and then stay on that path, right?"

"You got it!" Gus gave his daughter a peck on the cheek as the song ended.

For the rest of the night, Sarah watched Lily and Kurt enjoy their night dancing and laughing with friends and family.

When Kurt asked Sarah for a dance, she hadn't been surprised. Over the last five years, both he and Lily have shown Sarah love. The three of them spent many weekends enjoying their favorite movies together. Kurt always made Sarah laugh with his impressions and his ability to memorize movie lines.

"I know I can barely reach your chest, Kurt, but you better treat my baby right, or I will find you, and I will kill you," Sarah said with a smirk she couldn't contain.

In his best Armenian accent, he said, "Good luck."

They laughed as they reenacted her favorite line from their number one action movie. "I know we're joking, but I'm kinda serious."

"Don't worry, I'll be everything Lily wants and needs in a husband."

"I know you will be, thank you." Sarah's heart warmed with the promise of his words.

Kurt met Sarah's eyes. "I need to ask you something."

Whatever Kurt needed, she'd do her best to help.

"Will you please come to Africa with us? We could use your expertise with the kids."

Except that!

Sarah tipped her head back and laughed. "You'll be everything for Lily, even her strong arm when hers doesn't meet the mark."

It was Kurt's turn to laugh. "Both of us are very worried about you. I haven't said anything because it's never been my place. Now that I'm part of the family, I need you to know that Lily has been distraught for years as she watched you sink more and more into misery. Why won't you contact Brandon? It's evident to everyone that you both still love each other."

Still love each other? Sarah knew how she felt, but there was no way Brandon still loved her — Kurt must be delusional. Was it possible that Kurt had been in contact with Brandon recently? Maybe Kurt knew more than her. Before she could ask, Lily appeared from nowhere and stole her husband away.

Sarah had a lot of soul-searching to do. *Thank you, Lord, for this wonderful family who cares about me. Help me care about myself as much as they do. Please show me how you want me to go and give me the strength to stay on course.*

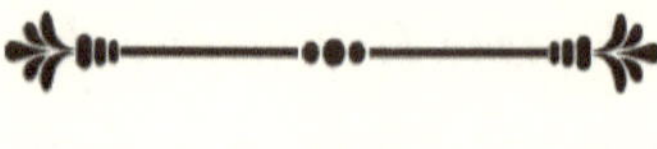

2

Brandon - Maine

A few more nails and Brandon could call it quits for the day. Taking on outside projects during the fall months in Maine can get pretty dicey. Thankfully, they'd had a pretty standard fall, hitting the mid-sixties, low seventies during the day, and fifties at night.

The sun slowly settled behind the tall pines, letting Brandon know he only had about an hour to finish the job and pick up his mess before darkness loomed over him.

The thought made one side of his lip curl up slightly. Darkness. Wasn't that what he'd lived in twenty-four-seven for the past five years? The last time he'd fully smiled was when Sarah accepted his marriage proposal. Sadly, the smile hadn't lasted long. She'd called it off as the ball had been about to drop on New Year's Eve. If his counting was accurate, he'd lived in a state of sadness for the past one thousand seven hundred forty-nine days . . . and counting.

To say he'd been brooding every moment of every day wasn't accurate. His feelings and thoughts ebbed and flowed. Most days, an ominous gray cloud hung over Brandon's head. When his mind drifted to memories of Sarah, proverbial raindrops from the gray cloud bounced off him. Since that fateful day, Brandon had buried himself in work. When he hadn't been completing a job for a customer, he'd been hidden away in the confines of his home. Somewhere in the abyss of his closet, he'd stored away anything that had reminded him of Sarah.

Even with his house stripped of all things Sarah, she'd habitually wormed her way into his brain. He wasn't safe anywhere. He'd spent more time than humanly healthy in his home gym to ease the pain that burned in his chest. The longing and emptiness had called his name day after day, tempting him to break down, but he hadn't given in to that pain.

Today, he hadn't been too bad concerning memories. Unless, of course, you counted the discussion on the podcast he listened to frequently. Brandon found that the noise from the talking kept him moving without sucking him into a more profound feeling of despair, unlike Music, which brought his pain to the surface too quickly. The host and his guest had been discussing the disadvantages of construction workers wearing wedding bands. Tragically, the guest lost his finger and wedding band in a work accident.

Staring at his left hand, the bare ring finger flashed like a neon sign reading "not married." Sarah had left him. Would he mind having only nine fingers? Not if that meant he'd married Sarah five years ago.

A buzzing in his pocket pulled Brandon from his thoughts of the road not taken. "Hey, Girlie, how's it feel to be married?" Brandon had kept in touch with Lily over the years.

"It feels great!" Kurt's voice filled the speaker before Lily could respond.

Brandon guffawed. "I bet it does."

"You're on speaker, Brandon," Lily informed him of the obvious.

"Congratulations. How'd the wedding go? Sorry, I couldn't come. Did you get my gift?" It wasn't that Brandon *couldn't* go; he wouldn't go. The idea of seeing Sarah in a beautiful dress accentuating her heart-shaped face, pale blue eyes, and blonde hair, pulled up in some fancy way, showing off her long slender neck that he'd snuggled into so many times before, sounded about as fun as missing a nail and hammering his thumb. The irony, Brandon realized, was that Sarah had given him the hammer he used daily, so the idea of the hammer inflicting physical pain upon him made sense. Using said hammer caused him to think about Sarah.

Every.

Single.

Day.

Maybe he should get rid of the hammer or store it away like he had everything else. Nah. He enjoyed, in a gut-twisting sort of way, feeling close to her, even if it was through a hammer.

"We did. Thank you." Lily responded with a hint of sadness. "We would have rather you be there to walk me down the aisle, but Kurt and I understand."

"Hey Brandon, we're calling for more selfish reasons." Kurt got to the point of the call. "We head to Africa tomorrow. We discovered they need male volunteers to work with native boys in their sports program. We think you'd be perfect for that. It's only two weeks."

"I don't know." Brandon ran his calloused hand through his hair before resting it under the bicep of his arm holding the phone.

His gaze swept across his customer's yard. He predicted that it would take another day to finish the job. He had no other major tasks that couldn't wait two weeks. Maybe a getaway to help others would be precisely what he needed.

"Brandon." Lily's soft voice interrupted his thoughts. "We'll understand if you say no, but it would—"

"—Why don't you have me building something or fixing something? Working with kids is your—" Brandon cut himself off. Even mentioning Sarah's name right now soured his stomach.

"That isn't the need for this mission. If you're willing, I'm sure there's a mission somewhere that could use your carpentry skills."

"Don't push your luck, Lil." He paused long enough for Lily to ask if he was still there.

"Yeah, I am." He let out a loud sigh. "I'll do it. Tell me what I need to know."

An ear-piercing squeal forced the phone from Brandon's ear. He'd forgotten how powerful Lily's excitement could get. That caused a pang of regret and despair to course through his chest. Not only had he missed out on Sarah these last five years, he'd missed out on Lily. She'd kept him informed as much as she could, but he never wanted Lily to feel like she was in the middle of his and Sarah's differences.

"We already have your ticket waiting for you at the airport." The mischievousness in Lily's voice wasn't lost on Brandon.

"Oh, really?" Brandon chuckled, not surprised. Whenever Lily expected someone to say no, she would set everything up for that person, hoping she'd eliminated every barrier. He wouldn't complain this time, as he disliked making travel arrangements.

Lily rambled off details about housing and transportation. Finally, she agreed to text him all the necessary flight information so he could wrap up for the evening. Brandon would have to start at six tomorrow morning to complete the job if he was going to leave in two days.

"See you in Africa, Brandon." Lily's enthusiasm sounded even more heightened, even for her.

As Brandon stored his tools in his trailer, a funny feeling came over Brandon that he couldn't quite place. Perhaps it was just nerves about flying to another continent. Brandon had never traveled outside of the United States. He and Sarah were going to Europe for their honeymoon. They'd also talked about traveling all over the world once Lily graduated. Maybe the thought of traveling without her, as his wife, rattled his senses.

Brandon made a mental list of everything to pack during the rush home. Passport. *Don't forget your passport*. He couldn't believe he would use it for the first time. . . and without Sarah. "Pack light," he recalled Kurt's advice. "One small suitcase is all you need. There's a place to wash clothes every fifth day, so you don't have to bring many."

Lily and Kurt were pros at mission trips. They'd started going on them as freshmen at The University of Florida at Gainesville. Brandon was proud when he thought of Lily and Kurt's great work for others. Witnessing the beginning of their relationship and seeing them now left him with the hope that love does win out ... sometimes.

After a quick dinner – thanks to his crockpot – of chili and rice, Brandon rummaged through his closet to find a duffle bag. Before discovering the bag, he stumbled upon a box. He jerked his hand back from the lid like it was an electric fence, ready to send jolts through his body. Burdened by the rectangular demon before him, he fell to his knees, wondering if he should open it. Once that lid came off, he knew the pain would fill the room like a genie being released from its lantern. Was he prepared to deal with what lay in that box? He didn't think so, but this was happening tonight for some reason.

Brandon was a 'rip the bandaid off quickly' kind of guy with everything except this. Gingerly, he held the box between his hands and stared at the box. Willing audible answers from God – *open (or don't open) the box, my child* – that he knew wouldn't come, but hoped for them anyway, believing God could answer him directly if He wanted.

Full disclosure – Brandon wanted to open the box. He wanted to feel the pain. Why? Heck, if he knew. Maybe that was so he wouldn't make the same mistake again. He realized, almost instantly, that it wasn't the pain he wanted to feel. He just wanted to see her, and the pain was an unfortunate result.

Brandon lifted the box's lid. The most beautiful blue eyes he'd ever seen stared back at him. They reminded him of the pictures he'd seen of water in Aruba- not the green depths of the water, but the top layer of light blue that captivates visitors instantly.

A frustrated groan escaped Brandon's throat. He picked up the small black velvet box. His fingers turned white with the pressure he infused on the destructive memory of what could have been. Setting that aside, Brandon sorted through the items — pictures of him and Sarah smiling and kissing burned through his core. The urge to fly to Florida instead of Africa weighed on him heavily. He'd thought about showing up on Sarah's doorstep many times. She'd gotten him to read a couple of romance novels with her back in the day, so his showing up out of the blue to fix their relationship didn't seem odd. Yet, he never did it, convincing himself that romance novels weren't real life. In reality, Sarah had left him, didn't think he was worthy enough to marry, and hashing that out didn't seem like a productive use of time.

Brandon released a deep breath, placing the cover back on the box and stuffing it in the far back corner of his closet. There, he found the bag he needed and started stuffing his clothes in by the fistful. He threw the bag on his bed and walked toward the bathroom to pack what he required. His foot kicked something. Bending down, he picked up the box housing the ring that should be on Sarah's finger. He tossed it in his bag with an envelope he'd kept from the box. Regret singed his core. He should have finished the letter and sent it years ago. Maybe this would be a good time. The strong connection he'd had to the past tonight wore on him.

Once he finished packing and settled into bed, a spark of anger hit Brandon. He'd already experienced most of the grief stages: denial, anger, bargaining, depression, and acceptance at some point, but he still struggled. He'd tried to accept the situation. He figured he'd accepted it by not doing anything to change it. As he tossed and turned, he thought about how, if he had sent the letter, things might be different now. One can never be sure, but it'd become evident that the anger, still flaring through his chest, was still present. He'd chosen long ago to snuff out the bad with good memories of Sarah. That was easy to do because he hadn't seen her to get closure. He can only imagine how he'd react if he ever came face to face with her again.

As he drifted off to sleep, Brandon realized how important this trip to Africa would be. Yeah, he would help the boys with their sports, but he also needed to help himself. This trip would finally allow him to move on from Sarah.

3

Sarah -Florida

To her surprise, Sarah missed a call from Lily. She hadn't expected to hear from her daughter until they returned from their mission trip. They'd said farewell at the wedding, knowing Lily and Kurt were leaving for Africa shortly after their nuptials.

"Climb Mt. Kilimanjaro for me," had been Sarah's final words to her daughter and new son-in-law as they left the reception last night. Sarah knew Lily's tactics. She thought she could convince Sarah to go with them if they promised to climb said mountain – one of Sarah's bucket list endeavors – even though people deem it the easiest of the seven summits.

This morning, Sarah had dragged herself out of bed, her mundane life calling. She pushed her stiff legs around the block for a five-mile run before the hot, humid Florida sun emerged, making her sticky and uncomfortable. Over the years, running had become even more prominent in her life. Not so much for the training but for the forgetting. As therapeutic as it might be, most of the time, it also presented its difficulty. At least once a week, she thought of how she and Brandon had met in Maine. Running the loop connecting her family's farm to the main road, she'd twisted her ankle. Brandon had carried her home. The thought of him carrying her anywhere – injured or otherwise – always made her smile. It never lasted long, as regret slapped her in the face, reminding her of what an idiot she'd been to walk away from him.

It would have been better to explain her desire for him and the guilt she had still harbored about moving on from Jake. Hindsight was twenty-twenty. Without a doubt left, she knew that Brandon would have worked with her – let her sort her feelings out or have a long engagement. Something. Anything. But she'd ended it all thinking, at the time, that it was easier to walk away and avoid the guilt.

She tried not to beat herself up too much. At the time, she'd prayed – endlessly – and felt God leading her to walk away. Her prayers since consisted of getting rid of unnecessary guilt and hoping Brandon would return to her. Sarah believed God's will played out in everyone's lives. She'd never thought of God as a wishing well, so perhaps if she wanted to reunite with Brandon, she'd have to do something to make it happen.

Now, Sarah sat on her screened-in porch, nursing a second glass of water since showering. Her phone rang. Lily's face filled the screen.

"Hey, honey. Sorry, I missed your call. Are you all packed for Africa?"

"You know it." Lily's high spirit made Sarah smile.

Lily was known for her determination. She could convince anyone to do anything, which made Sarah question the purpose of her daughter's call.

"Mom, I'm offering you the opportunity of a lifetime." Without giving Sarah a chance to speak, Lily argued her point further. "The kids in Africa need you. Will you please reconsider coming with us?"

"I don't know, Lily..."

"You'll stay with the same host family as Kurt and me. You get to work with kids, live in the flesh again. You teach 'em. We heal 'em."

Sarah couldn't imagine how difficult it was for them to be in med school and try to heal the world. They talked about joining Doctors Without

Borders when they finished, which didn't surprise Sarah, but she'd be lying if she said she didn't mind them being so far away all the time.

"Getting away will do you some good, Mom. Maybe you'll stop beating yourself up over the past."

Sarah's next round of students wasn't starting until the new year. The only thing holding her back from doing something good was herself. Perhaps a couple weeks in another country would help her to stop feeling sorry for herself and remember that there are worse things in life than a broken – no, demolished – heart.

"What do I have to do?" Sarah let out a breath.

"Really? Mom, you won't regret this!" Lily squealed. "The team leader will pick you up at the airport. Your ticket will be waiting for you at the check-in tomorrow morning. Be there by six a.m. Your flight leaves at eight-thirty. I'll text you the check-in gate number when we hang up."

"I should have known that you would have everything planned perfectly. But so that you know, I think you're a shameless shark ... preying on my desire to help children. What am I going to do with you?" Sarah's quick chuckle revealed her playfulness.

As Sarah boarded the plane for the final leg of this ridiculously long flight, an incoming call from Lily appeared on the screen. "Hey, Girlie. I'm settling into my seat now."

"Yay. I can't wait to see you. Kurt and I will pick you up at the airport instead of a team leader. Mom, there's been a bit of a mix-up, and you'll have to—"

"—Ladies and gentlemen, this is your captain speaking." Sarah pulled the phone away from her ear. "We've been asked to wait a little longer as a group of people from a delayed connecting flight are getting their tickets scanned for this flight. It is the final trip of the day to Mt. Kilimanjaro airport. I appreciate your patience."

Putting the phone back to her ear, Sarah sighed. "We've been delayed. We're waiting on a group of late arrivals."

"That's okay, Mom. I'm sure it will be worth it."

What did that mean? Sarah didn't like her daughter's tone. As a teenager, she'd always known when Lily was up to something. Her pitch got an octave higher, and her singsong tone was extra sweet, just like now. What did she know that Sarah didn't? Sarah was afraid to ask.

"See you in a few hours. Love you, Mom." She hung up quickly.

A gazillion questions ran through Sarah's mind. Namely, what were Lily and Kurt conjuring up? Hopefully, there wasn't anything wrong with her volunteering. Why wouldn't the leader be meeting her at the airport? She wouldn't worry about that right now. Instead, Sarah would get some shut-eye and pray that no one sat beside her on this flight. On her trip here, she had to listen to the grumpy man next to her complaining nonstop about the child behind him while the mother tried her hardest to keep the child quiet. Sarah stood and shut the overhead compartment, hoping no one would stuff anything else in there with her carry-on.

Dealing with adults was definitely more challenging than with children. Maybe that's why Sarah enjoyed teaching, both in the brick-and-mortar style and online. The younger ones, like the one on the plane, were her favorite. They were honest and genuine. Sarah could teach them new things, and their eyes would light up. Adults were hard to read, standoffish, and too secretive. She knew that all too well. In fact, she had been accused of being all those things at one time or another.

"Ah." Settled in her seat, Sarah tried to get comfortable for the last three and a half hours of this thirty-one-hour trip. Exhaustion raided her body. She'd never understood why flights flew past people's destinations to layover for hours before flying back to their desired destination.

Being in Qatar hadn't bothered Sarah, but as she squeezed her eyes shut, she was happy to relax in her first-class seat. The spacious seat felt like a big puffy cloud on her back and legs, dismissing whatever problem might await her at the mission site. Her eyes slowly shut.

"Woo hoo!" Roars and cheers startled Sarah. They were still sitting on the tarmac. *How long has it been?* Sarah heard the commotion in the plane's general seating area, announcing the late passengers' arrival. *Finally, we can get moving.* Sarah looked at her watch – fifteen minutes past the scheduled departure time. She'd never heard of planes waiting around for people, but she wasn't a frequent flier either. She wasn't complaining, though. If she had been part of this group, she'd want people to wait for her. Elated that they'd leave soon, she repositioned herself to return to la-la land.

She let her mind wander as she stared out the miniature window. Moments later, the flight attendant pulled her from her thoughts. "Right here, sir." The blonde stewardess stood, pointing to the empty seat next to Sarah. "Enjoy your flight."

Sarah's eyes caught sight of the most handsome man alive. Her jaw hinged open, and her mouth instantly dried up like the Sahara. This woman lost all control. Her rapid heartbeat and breathing grew exponentially. Sarah shivered. Her clammy arms and hands had her wishing for a sweatshirt. Then, like a drop thrill ride, her heart plummeted into her stomach. *Where are those little barf bags?* She desperately needed one, as her nerves were getting the best of her. As the man approached the seat, time seemed to stand still. *I had said my prayers this morning; maybe He was in a joking mood. No, this is a dream, right, Lord?* Sarah pinched herself. *Nope.* She was fully awake and unprepared. Fear and excitement ransacked her body.

Maybe all her daydreams were finally coming to fruition. Maybe his proximity would force her to do what she should have done years ago. Maybe, just maybe, God was answering her prayers.

"H-Hi Brandon."

$$4$$

Brandon squeezed his eyes shut, counted to three and opened his eyes again. *Yup. She's still there. Lord, help me.* He approached the seat the friendly flight attendant would like him to sit in, never taking his eyes off Sarah. Man, he had missed her. *No, no, no! Do not think like that. She is the woman who ripped out your heart and stomped on it five years ago!*

Air. He needed Air. The rise and fall of Brandon's chest quickened. He grabbed the back of the empty seat. A memory of Sarah standing on the porch as he drove away right after she broke up with him came flooding back. He could not sit next to her for the next few hours.

"Do you have any other seats on the plane?" Brandon deadpanned.

"Ouch," he heard Sarah whisper as she broke eye contact. "Dear Lord, please help me," she murmured.

What did she need help with? She's the reason we're not married. Frustration bubbled in his chest. Brandon tried to stop loving her over the years. He should have been over her by now, but he wasn't.

The stewardess shook her head. "Sorry, Sir. The flight is full." She stood there, waiting for Brandon to do or say something.

He sighed. It wasn't this woman's fault that God enjoyed playing around like this. Brandon had prayed earlier for closure, but this was not what he intended. Didn't God know him at all?

Sarah had refused to marry Brandon five long years ago, leaving him in a state of despair until he forced himself to function again. Under no circumstance would he fall under her spell again. The immense pain that sometimes hit him like a hot poker now simmered in his gut.

Then, something occurred to Brandon. Focusing his attention on the stewardess again. "Is Tanzania the final destination of this flight?"

"Yes, Sir, it is." The woman, who looked four or five years younger than Brandon, smiled broadly.

Suspicion swirled in his stomach. Had Lily and Kurt set him up? Is this why he was working with kids and not using his professional skills? He'd let his guilt for not attending their wedding and desire to move on dictate his decision to accept the mission trip despite his brief, initial reservations. He had to admit that after hearing about how he would be helping kids learn how to play sports, he'd felt a strong tug at his soul to go on this mission.

A fire burned in his chest. *If Lily and Kurt set me up, they must have set up Sarah, too. Or, is it possible that she knew I'd be here and wanted to see me?* A pang of excitement ratcheted up in his body. *Steady, man. It's not likely. She broke your heart once. Don't let her do it again. You've moved on.*

A vicious cackle pierced his inner ear. He hadn't moved on; he'd only coped. She didn't need to know that, though. *How much does she know?* Gus had promised to keep the details to a minimum when he spoke with her, but Brandon knew Gus. He'd been playing reporter between the two of them for years. Learning everything he could about Sarah made his heart sing, so he didn't care what Gus told her; he'd made it clear that no matter how much he loved his daughter, Gus was the captain of Team Brandon.

He and Sarah had not spoken – not one word – since she walked away. Yet here they were, stuck on a plane together for hours. Sarah was more beautiful than she had been five years ago. *Knock it off. Don't let her know you still care.*

At least Sarah's remarkable blue eyes looked as nervous as he felt. Her previously dropped jaw had found its way home. Fortunately, a little bit of color had resurfaced in her cheeks. The light pink hue had drained from her face when their gazes had initially locked. He'd worried, for a brief moment, that Sarah was going to pass out.

"Thank you," Brandon said to the flight attendant as he lifted the overhead compartment, shoved his bag in, and forcefully shut the door.

Brandon took a deep breath, trying to calm himself before speaking to the woman who had broken his heart. "H-Hey," he said, pausing briefly when he heard the tautness in his voice. He wiped his palms on his jeans as he settled in his seat. Brandon ran his fingers through his hair, casually wiping the sweat that had formed at his hairline. A pit the size of an ostrich's egg weighed his stomach down. Sarah had been everything to him.

That made it even harder. He couldn't stop staring at her flawless face, full lips, and thick blonde hair that cascaded down her back. She was exquisite. He didn't remember her being this thin, though. The mental picture he had recalled for the last five years had been sweet and tortuous but nothing compared to her in the flesh. For the next three or four hours, he needed willpower and Superman's laser focus to avoid letting Sarah take hold of his heart any more than she already had. Then, he could go on his mission while Sarah fulfilled hers.

Once the wheels secured underneath the plane, Sarah asked, "Where are you headed? I didn't think you'd ever fly out of the country."

Brandon couldn't believe the nerve of this woman. "Seriously? Are you under the delusion that you can click your heels and we transport ourselves to five years ago?"

"I'm trying to talk with you," Sarah's voice was sheepish.

Brandon shook his head and scoffed. "I don't talk to strangers on planes." He hadn't been on a plane in over a decade, so he didn't know if that was a true statement, but the v formation her brows were making revealed that she got the impact of that punch.

So much for being strong. A force stronger than him poked him in the chest. *You're here to get closure, so make it happen. Talk to her.* What was he worried about? Once he started talking, he knew it would be just like old times. How could it not? He loved – loves – this woman.

"I'm meeting Lily and Kurt in Africa for a mission trip." Brandon didn't expect his voice to sound so sweet. He wanted to be angry, or at the very least grumpy – she needed to understand the pain she'd caused. But how could he? He wasn't angry. He was devastated – she left him.

"I'm also working on a mission trip with Lily and Kurt." Her honeyed voice made his pulse race.

This was definitely not what he'd expected. "You left Sarah. You refused to take my calls. You moved back to Florida. You've ghosted me for the last five years." He pushed the exasperated words out slowly. "If you think we're going to pick up right where we left off, you are sadly mistaken." Her lip started to tremble. *That's not fair; don't you dare!* She knew he'd melt like frosty right now if she started crying.

Sarah closed her eyes and inhaled. As she slowly released her breath, she clasped her hands on her lap and rapidly ran one thumb over the other, a telltale sign that she was nervous. "I'm sorry I upset you. The shock of seeing you made me want to know how you've been doing."

"I'm fine." He lied. lad

Sarah stared straight ahead. "You sound it."

"Not sure what you expected." Brandon's stomach tightened. He'd waited for this moment a long time. She needed to explain herself.

Sarah grinned and blew a puff of breath out her nose. "Knowing my daughter, she's set this all up. I'm sorry. She'll be lucky if I don't hop on the next flight and return home to prove that she shouldn't meddle in other people's lives."

Brandon froze. Obviously, the only thing that bothered her was that Lily and Kurt outsmarted them. Being trapped in this situation wasn't his idea of fun, but a part of him — a big part — was excited to be next to the love of his life. He might thank Lily and Kurt for making this happen...maybe. Confused emotions drained his energy.

Silence assaulted the space between them.

Brandon's leg bounced up and down rapidly. He couldn't wait any longer. A barrage of questions spewed from his mouth. "Maybe she realized it was about time you explained yourself? Why'd you really break our engagement? How come you wouldn't talk to me? Did you really need to move back to Florida? Do you still love me? Are you—"

"—Ladies and gentlemen, this is your captain speaking. We are approaching twenty thousand feet. When we reach thirty thousand, the seatbelt light will be turned off, but we encourage you to stay in your seat in case of any unforeseen events."

Sarah opened her mouth to respond, but the captain's announcement stopped her. Brandon honestly didn't care what the pilot had to say. He would finally get answers from the woman sitting next to him. This was so surreal. He'd wanted this for so long, but now that it was here, anxiousness filled his heart.

Sarah reached out, placing her hand on his forearm. He flinched, pulling his arm away. She hung her head and wrapped her arms around her midsection. An outsider would think her touch repulsed him when, in fact, a jolt of electricity shot through him. He wouldn't bother explaining that, though. There was no point in sharing how much she still affected him.

Brandon studied Sarah's face. Her longing glance weakened his resolve to keep his distance. She licked her lips. *Don't do that, Sarah.* Was she seriously considering kissing him right now? Probably not. Would he kiss her? Probably. Her sparkly blue eyes were unreadable. He reached for her hand but quickly retracted it and shoved both hands under his biceps. Keeping his arms crossed was the only way he knew they'd keep to themselves.

Sarah's familiar wildberry fragrance, though faint, teased his senses. He'd missed her through and through. Without a doubt, Sarah was his Kryptonite. *Be strong. Tell her the damage she has caused.* "I can't do this." Brandon leaned forward, resting his elbows on his knees. He dropped his head into his palms. Out of the corner of his eye, he saw Sarah reach out her hand. She pulled it back quicker, probably due to her first failed attempt. His shoulder or back, wherever she'd intended on resting her slender palm, yearned for her comforting touch.

"You gutted me, Sarah. Your dad has kept me well informed, as I'm sure he has you. It's been a double-edged sword, though. As much as I've wanted to know everything going on with you, it killed me that I wasn't part of it."

"I'm sorry." Sarah's voice, barely above a whisper.

Turning his head toward Sarah but still resting his palm on his forehead, Brandon asked, "If you're sorry, then why are we here like this?" Brandon shook his head. "Never mind." Brandon leaned back into the seat, resting his head, and looked toward the ceiling.

Pulling her bottom lip between her teeth, Sarah sighed. "I'm sorry we're here." She stared out the micro-sized window.

He didn't want to hear sorry. Brandon's head felt like it would explode any second. He'd finally gotten his chance to confront Sarah, and he couldn't. "Are you working with kids too?" Brandon asked nervously.

"I'm not sure of anything anymore." Sarah shrugged. "Lily called while we were waiting for you and the rest of the group. She and Kurt will pick me up at the airport. Some problem came up with the volunteer, I guess."

"Interesting." Brandon ran his hand over his face. "Lily and Kurt are picking me up at the airport too."

No, no, no. This wasn't good. I cannot spend the next two weeks with my ex-fiancé, who still has my heart in a vice grip, and then return to Maine with her fifteen hundred miles away in Florida. To keep his walls in place, he needed sleep.

"I'm beat." Brandon reclined his seat, shut his eyes, and pretended to sleep, feeling Sarah's gaze burning his skin. *Could it be possible that Sarah still had feelings for him?* The longing he'd seen in her eye let him think it was possible, but it wasn't something he could deal with right now. *She could not still love me when she hadn't reached out or tried to talk to me in five years.*

"Remember, I know you well enough to know you're fake sleeping," Sarah stated dryly, waiting for Brandon to respond. He never did.

She doesn't know me anymore. Lord, keep my eyes shut no matter what she does to entice me. Please. She's always been into proving points; help me prove one to her.

"Oh goodness! Look at that lightning," Sarah shrieked. "I hope we don't get struck." The plane shook. The ding for the seatbelt sign turned back on.

Why, Lord, couldn't you be on Team Brandon right now? It took Brandon's restraint to keep his eyes closed during the turbulence. He didn't want to hear Sarah's story tonight.

The plane rumbled. Sarah grabbed onto Brandon's arm. Electricity filled the first-class cabin. "Sorry." Sarah's soft tone warmed him throughout.

When Brandon didn't respond, Sarah began praying. "Lord, please keep everyone safe. Give the pilots the wisdom they need to fly us safely to Africa." She put the armrest between them up and shifted. She pulled one leg up, placing it on the seat under the other leg. "Please let him forgive me. Please supply me with the strength I need to get through this mission. Amen."

As the plane landed, Brandon bounced in his seat, shocked he'd given in to his pretend sleeping. The blanket that had been covering his arms fell to the floor. He picked it up with a questioning look toward Sarah.

"You had goosebumps. I tried to cover you with my sweatshirt, but it didn't stretch. You've... expanded a bit..." he caught her eyes roaming over his arms and chest. Stifling a grin, he wondered if she felt the sizzling attraction between them or if that was only in his head. He wouldn't lie; her interest in his physique made his heart leap. "...so I asked the flight attendant to get the blanket for you." Sarah shrugged like it was no big deal and turned slightly toward the window.

Emotion clogged his throat. No one, except his mother, had ever been that thoughtful of his needs before. This was just one more example of why he loved Sarah so much. She thought of him even now.

Being this close to Sarah had played with his mind. Her profile revealed the same sadness and questioning he felt within. The lingering fear of being rejected – again – was too intense for him to hand his heart back over to Sarah willingly, but would he be able to stop it?

His dad had always told him, "Son, we learn through pain or insight." Right now, he felt like he'd learn through both. He wasn't strong enough to learn through any more pain, so the best thing to do was stay away – far away – from Sarah.

5

The hibernating butterflies in Sarah's stomach had stirred up and wreaked havoc the entire flight. Unfortunately, their reunion hadn't gone as she'd imagined. According to her daydreams, she would express her declaration of love, which would be well received.

But, instead of a warm embrace or a kiss to seal their reconciliation, Brandon had fallen asleep to avoid her. She knew he had pretended to sleep at first. Even the storm hadn't stirred him from his fake nap to finish the conversation they had started. She'd been right to think that Brandon wouldn't want to hear from her after she dropped the bombshell on him that she couldn't marry him and then moved away.

The intense way he used to look at her, making her entire body tingle, wasn't as alluring as it once had been. Anguish. That was what she saw in his eyes now.

She had fallen victim to his scent again — the same mahogany-vanilla cologne that had once captivated her.

What had she expected? Brandon wasn't going to let her off the hook easily. She would have to fix this since she's the one who broke it. The last five years had given her all the time necessary to work through the guilt she'd harbored about moving on after her husband's fatal accident.

She'd finally realized that Jake would never begrudge her an opportunity to be happy, especially with a man like Brandon – the one she used to know. The way he'd once looked at her, enticed her with his sweet words, protected her, and listened to her revealed his respect and adoration.

Snap out of it! He's not into you anymore. You lost your chance. Move on. The awkwardness of this situation wore on Sarah. Like a ping pong match, her thoughts ricocheted back and forth off the sides of her brain. She wanted to wake him up and beg for forgiveness, but the opposite side convinced her that he needed space. That seemed comical to her since they'd had over eighteen hundred days of space. The sight of him flooded her with desire. She didn't want more space, but it was her turn to respect whatever he decided.

The current silence and the blank look on Brandon's face as she explained why he had a blanket crushed her hope that he'd be open to a new start. Again, it was her fault. She would complete her mission, focus on whatever God wanted her to experience, and return to Florida.

Sarah found herself getting lost in her regrets, lambasting her past decisions. Guilt and despair had eaten away at her the morning after she'd called the wedding off. She'd realized her colossal mistake but didn't do anything to fix it. Call it pride, anxiety, or doubt; it didn't matter now. Sarah wondered if Brandon would be open to starting over or if he'd moved on.

When the pilot released the seatbelt sign, they stood simultaneously, grazing each other. She inhaled sharply. It was impossible to keep her emotions in check.

Brandon towered over her with a grin, probably realizing the effect he was having on her. He'd always been observant and enjoyed making her squirm. His nearness distracted her as she attempted to retrieve her carry-on from the overhead compartment. She felt his breath on the side of her neck, producing ripples down her spine and causing her to shiver.

"Are you cold?" Brandon's deep, husky voice pierced her ears.

"No, but could you back up a bit, please?" Sarah pulled her bottom lip between her teeth, unable to focus on anything except Brandon's cologne filling her senses as he leaned over her shoulder to make eye contact.

"Sorry, no can do. Tight quarters." Sarah thought he chuckled like he enjoyed torturing her.

Jerk!

"Here, let me help you." He stepped closer. *How was that even possible?* His hard chest pressed against Sarah's back as he retrieved her bag. If she didn't know better, he lingered longer than necessary. Maybe his nap gave him the ability to forgive her? She hoped so.

Peeling her eyes open, she whispered, "Thank you." She put the strap over her shoulder and moved toward the plane's exit.

"What are you doing? Are you seriously going to walk away from me again?" Brandon snatched his bag and rushed to catch up.

Never slowing her pace, Sarah apologized. "I just wanted to get off the plane quickly." That was the truth. She didn't need to tell him that she was a light-year away from making her fantasies of kissing him a reality. Would one small kiss of gratitude hurt? Don't most women kiss the handsome man for helping retrieve her bag from the overhead compartment? No! Of course, they don't – not when it doesn't feel welcomed. Sarah was thoroughly enamored with his man, which could only mean one thing. Trouble.

As they waited for Sarah's luggage at the carousel, she looked around for Lily. Now that they'd landed, she wanted to know the problem with her volunteering and what the two newlyweds conjured up for her and Brandon.

Amazingly, Sarah wasn't mad with Lily and Kurt; not really. She knew their intentions came from a loving place. Truthfully, she should thank them for forcing her to do what she should have done years ago, but she wouldn't encourage their sneakiness.

What she said next could either help her or hurt her when it came to Brandon. It bothered her how he'd seemed so distant before he'd *'fallen asleep.'* Then, once he'd woken up, he was trying to be sweet and getting too close for her comfort. Now, they stood in silence again. Her mind was already shot. His hot and cold temperament wouldn't bode well for her, given her lack of sleep – she was bound to snap.

"Excuse me." Sarah forced a smile. Leaving a ribbon on her suitcase was smart. It helped her retrieve it quickly. Wrapping two hands on the fabric handle of her overstuffed rectangle, she hoisted it off the silver sphere. It plopped to the ground. Sarah pulled the retractable handle up and dragged it behind her.

You can do this, Sarah. Stop fantasizing about Brandon. You lost your chance with him when you called off the engagement, so suck it up, help the people of this country, and enjoy your time with Lily and Kurt.

Sarah's pep talk to herself didn't last long. She rolled her suitcase back to him. "May I?" Brandon pointed at the suitcase handle. Sarah's heart melted. As she handed over the suitcase, their fingers brushed. A longing sigh escaped from her lungs when the encounter ended too quickly. Pain radiated from Sarah's chest, watching Brandon's muscles flex when he did a bicep curl with his duffle bag and twisted it over his shoulder. *Wow.* On so many levels. Her lungs searched for much-needed oxygen. She appreciated the scene unfolding in front of her. The most impressive thing about Brandon was that he didn't know how handsome and alluring he was.

"Mom! Brandon!"

Sarah spun to see Lily running towards them. They embraced, acting like they hadn't seen each other in years despite it having been only four days.

"Man, I hope I get that kind of greeting someday." Kurt quipped.

Lily half turned to face her husband but kept her arm around her mom. "When you leave for four days, I'll welcome you home in style."

His eyes widened, causing the newlyweds to laugh.

"Alright, that's more information than a mother needs." Sarah took a step back. "Changing the subject, I'm not happy with either of you."

"Us?" They questioned in unison, with the cat that ate the canary look on their faces.

Sarah pulled her daughter off to the side, just out of earshot.

"You intentionally put Brandon on this trip with me. He sat next to me on the plane. Please tell me I do not have to work with him for the next two weeks."

Silence.

"Lily, I'm not joking. I can't deal," Sarah said, frowning and placing her hands on her hips.

Brandon and Kurt joined the ladies with Sarah's suitcase at his feet. "Well, matchmaker one, your mom said there was a problem with the volunteer site." Brandon's voice had a little bite to it, but Sarah knew how much Brandon loved Lily.

"Are you both ready to go?" Lily hugged Brandon but ignored his question.

Sarah separated the two. "Lily, what's going on."

Lily's eyes darted to Kurt's. He nodded at her as he wrapped his arms around her to give her the courage to speak.

She finally spits out her plan. "I thought you'd be able to help us with the kids in the clinic, but there isn't any more room in the volunteer's house, so instead, we've moved you to the school to work with kids."

Sarah turned her head toward Brandon. "Aren't you volunteering at a school?"

He shrugged. "That's what I was told."

"You're both at the same school," Lily mumbled.

Brandon crossed his arms over his chest, making his biceps bulge, distracting Sarah. "So we're working at the same school. I'm working with kids, which is not my expertise — this sounds like a setup, big time."

"There's more." Lily shrugged her shoulders and lifted her pointer finger.

"Spit it out." Sarah glanced at her daughter.

"The volunteer housing is all filled, too."

"We have a solution, though," Kurt said, relieving Lily. "We've got a tent real close to the house that you can stay in while you're here. It's only fifteen days. The weather is still nice. You two can handle it, right?"

"Two?" Brandon bleated. "There isn't room for me either?"

Lily shook her head.

This cannot be happening. I haven't seen Brandon for the past five years, and now we have to share a tent for two weeks. Lord, are you kidding me? Why did I come here again? I think you made a mistake — big, huge, colossal. Please fix it.

Brandon cleared his throat. "If there isn't anything we can do, we'll just have to make the best of it," he said, shrugging his shoulders as they walked out of the airport.

Sarah couldn't believe how calm he was about this. Her insides were gearing up for Armageddon. What happened to the anxious man who'd fallen asleep on the plane? He'd been replaced with this new, placid version, making Sarah leery.

"Over here," Lily hollered, pulling her from her anxiousness.

When they reached the car, Brandon stopped at the backseat and opened the door for Sarah. "I could have gotten that myself." *Yup, her nerves were shot. Be nice,* Sarah coached herself.

"I think 'thank you' are the words you meant." Brandon waited for her to sit in the car.

Staring up at the man, full of class, Sarah's stomach swirled. She loved that he was a gentleman, but it just made things even harder for her if he was going to shut her out. "Thank you."

A charming grin slowly grew on his lips. "You're welcome." Attraction burst through her veins. It should be illegal to smile like that.

For a brief moment, it looked like he had removed some of the walls he had built around himself. Maybe she and Brandon could pick up where they had left off.

6

Brandon wasn't upset with Lily and Kurt, per se. They'd convinced him that neither of them had planned on Sarah and Brandon sharing a living space for the next few weeks. Yet here they were, sharing air way too close for comfort. Had he known he'd be stuffed in a sardine-sized tent with the woman he'd longed for, he would have chosen to stay home and hammer nails into his skin.

In the spirit of forgiveness and being on another continent, Brandon had made a conscious decision during his fake nap to give this situation to God and let Him make things happen. That seemed better than him taking matters into his own hands.

They'd go through their eight-hour training tomorrow before starting with the kids the following day. Right now, a more significant problem loomed over them. The tent they would have to share for the next two weeks only held one person.

"You're joking, right?" Sarah snapped. "Thank goodness Lily and Kurt let me borrow this backpack and stored my luggage with them. We'd never fit it in there." Sarah pointed at the tight tunnel they'd sleep in the next few weeks.

"*We'll* barely fit in there. Must be why Kurt told me to pack light." His gaze held hers for a moment too long.

Brandon was half-tempted to let her stay here alone. He could figure something else out. *Didn't she realize this wasn't a walk in the park for him, either?* This woman tore his heart out, stomped on it, and left it for dead. He was still picking up the pieces.

His inner spirit spoke. *Breathe.* Familiar words from the Book of Jeremiah replayed in his mind. *"For I know the plans I have for you," declares the LORD, "plans to prosper you and not to harm you, plans to give you hope and a future."*

Why, suddenly, was he thinking of comforting her right now? Brandon never heard Sarah bark like that before. He still loved her. Could she be his future? *Oh no, I'm not going through that again.*

None of that mattered right now. His primary concern was securing themselves inside this tent before nightfall so millions of gnats wouldn't eat them alive.

"I'm sorry for snapping. I guess I'm just still in shock. Anyway, I'm sorry, you didn't deserve that."

Brandon knelt on the ground to secure the tent's corners. "I feel the same way, so I get it. Apology accepted. Will you pull on that corner?"

"Sure."

It didn't take long to get the way-too-small tent ready for their first night. "We should get inside for the night. The natives said bugs are awful when the sun goes down," Brandon held the tent flap open.

Sarah grabbed her backpack. "I'm going to the bathroom. I'll be right back."

Most women wouldn't use an outhouse. In fact, most women his buddies had told him about wouldn't even be on this trip. Sarah was special.

What the past five years with Sarah would have been like invaded Brandon's thoughts. He felt robbed. She had stolen his happiness the day she called off the engagement. How could they spend the next fifteen days together pretending that hadn't happened?

While Sarah was gone, Brandon changed into a pair of athletic shorts. He never thought twice about the fact he doesn't wear a shirt to bed, until now. He hoped he wouldn't make Sarah feel uncomfortable. If this troubled Sarah, he'd wear a shirt and take the discomfort.

When he heard Sarah approach the tent, he lay close to the edge, knowing she wouldn't have enough room to enter if he hadn't.

When she opened the flap on the tent, he captured her eyes for a second before hers raked over the situation. "Dear God, please help me. I can't do this."

Brandon felt a slight smile tug at his lips. "What's wrong?"

"You need a shirt."

Propping up on his elbow, Brandon explained, "I never wear a shirt, but I'll put a tank top on if it will make you feel better."

He could see her contemplating her options as she crawled fully inside and secured the tent for the night. She knelt by the door flap and pulled a sweatshirt from her bag. "I'll just put this on so you can be comfortable."

"I don't mind, Sarah. I'd do anything for you." The words slipped out before he could stop them.

"Ditto," she whispered as she pulled the sweatshirt over her head.

"Except marry me." Brandon needed to get ahold of his tongue and shut it down for the evening. "Sorry, I should have said that."

Her expression of pity or sadness nearly suffocated him. "I should have married you. I wanted to, but I couldn't."

He'd lived with the thought that If he'd only been good enough, nothing would have stopped her. He couldn't trust her.

"How?" She gestured toward the remaining space in the tent. "Where do you want me?"

At my home as my wife. He couldn't say that. It wasn't his plan to make her feel bad about her past decision the entire time they volunteered.

"I think we'll be spooning. That's all there's room for," Brandon said, scooting his back against the tent. His heart raced at the thought of being so close to Sarah.

The trepidation he saw on her face rippled through his entire body. Sarah stretched out in front of him. His right arm was trapped between the ground and Sarah's back. She lifted her head multiple times before settling down.

"Are you good?"

"Yeah. I'm not squishing you, am I?" He barely heard Sarah's soft, shaky voice.

Brandon was so close to Sarah that he could smell her wildberry perfume, causing his pulse to pick up. "If anyone squishes anyone, it will be me crushing you. I'm apologizing in advance."

"You have gotten bigger. Did you start lifting weights, or is that all from working?"

The gallant question made Brandon smile. Sarah always said what was on her mind.

"I need something to take my mind off. . . life, so I lift a lot." He rested his top hand on her hip. He heard her suck in a breath and hold it.

He rocked her hip back and forth with this hand and squeezed his lips tight to keep the chuckle bubbling in his throat from escaping. "If you don't breathe, you die," he said light-heartedly.

Sarah quietly let out her breath. "I'm sorry. I need to find another place to sleep."

"As uncomfortable as this is for both of us, we must be grateful we have this tent." The only thing that made Brandon uncomfortable was the tension. Had they been married, sharing this tent could have been ... a lot more fun.

Sarah sighed. "I know you're right. Maybe we should clear the air, so—"

"—I don't think you want to hear what I say." Brandon cut her off.

"Maybe not, but we need to."

Brandon changed the subject. "Did you hear what the host told everyone tonight?"

"Yeah. Stay with a buddy. There have been five cheetah attacks in the last two months." Sarah sighed. "I'm more nervous about the human attacks."

She was referring to the recent attacks against Christian natives. The host revealed that over half of the population is Christian; however, the entire Tanzanian coast is populated by Muslims. They persecute the Christians and try to take control of the area. Additionally, many tribal groups resist the Word, making them groups to beware of.

Brandon's heart bled for these people. Although they knew victory would be theirs one day, the taste of defeat surrounded them here on earth. Just last week, a group of native girls traveling to get water for their family were beaten to within an inch of their lives for singing a hymn and saying 'God Bless you' to a newcomer.

When he agreed to come here, Brandon hadn't thought about danger. Moving on from the pain Sarah inflicted upon him and helping the kids here were his only motivations. Now, after hearing about the most recent attacks, he had to worry about keeping Sarah safe. It didn't matter to him if she still didn't think he was good enough; her fingers were vise grips around his heart, and he'd do whatever it took to protect her.

"Brandon." His name sounded sweet as saccharine on her lips. "Can we please talk?"

Tension filled his chest. "Look, the only reason you're even in this tent is because Lily guilted you into this mission trip; it's not because you wanted to reconnect with me." Brandon's harsh tone vibrated off the tent walls. "Let's not do this on the first night." Brandon continued, "Sleep well; tomorrow's a busy day."

Before speaking to Sarah about the past, he must clear his mind. Hurt still pierced his heart. He loved her without a doubt, but could he trust her? No, not yet. He did trust in God, though.

Tonight, Brandon silently thanked the Lord for this mission trip and prayed for protection over the people. He knew being in Africa would help him heal, one way or another. He'd heard of God having a dying family member hang on just long enough for the surviving members to come to terms with the death. Maybe God was on Team Brandon? These next couple of weeks with Sarah might be God's way to pull him from the death he'd wrapped around himself since she'd left.

Having Sarah in his arms again felt amazing. Her back resting against his bare chest produced a forest fire blazing out of control. Who was he kidding? This was the sweetest torture he'd ever experienced. If he wasn't careful, his heart could flatline. Would he ever be enough for Sarah?

7

The day of orientation and training was a killer. Being squished in a room with a dark-haired, handsome man with this much muscle should be illegal. Admittedly, it would have been fun if that man hadn't tried his hardest to act like she wasn't sitting right next to him breathing in his cologne, praying her heart didn't stop. Sarah lost focus many times. She secretly urged him to "accidentally" graze her arm or whisper something, anything in her ear like the couple behind them on their first mission trip.

Time with Brandon had not been going the way Sarah hoped it would. She wanted to clear the air and move on — whatever that might look like. Brandon had refused multiple times. Most recently, he'd abruptly shut the conversation down and raced to sleep, probably pretending again. Her heart melted when he sounded concerned about her safety. It was a bit nerve-racking thinking about the natives dying as martyrs, standing up for their belief, faith, and trust in Jesus Christ. Sarah always said that she would profess her belief in Jesus if ever put in a situation like these people are faced with daily, but no one knows what they will do in a situation until that time comes. She prayed the time never came.

Fortunately, these precious children kept Sarah's mind occupied mostly. Schools ran differently in Tanzania than they did in the States. Sarah already knew that, but it didn't ease her aching heart. Learning that only about thirty percent of kids got to attend lower secondary school made her heart cry. Most eighth, ninth, tenth, and eleventh graders couldn't afford to attend school. Instead, they risked their lives in mines or quarries. Sadly, many of them fall to tribal gangs or worse. After hearing this, a wave of nausea plowed through Sarah.

"These kids face many hardships. The aftermath may or may not spill over into their time with you." Fardowsa, the coordinator, relayed the information like she was ordering at a fast food joint. "Do not get involved. I know that sounds awful, but life is different here than in the States."

The woman's flip-flops slapped against the bottom of her foot as she paced around the room. "You must be vigilant when it comes to gangs, tribal or otherwise, and of course, beware of rebels. Your hosts should have already shared the most recent news with you." Fardowsa dropped her chin briefly before pulling her shoulders back and standing proudly. "You all have a target on your back. You're here to spread the word of Christ with these children. Our biggest foe is trying to take over this region, making all schools and businesses Muslim-owned and operated. They will not hesitate to kill you or the family you travel with. You need to let God lead every interaction with the kids."

Brandon glanced at Sarah from the corner of his eye and rested his hand on hers, his palm a cocoon for her hand. She knew how hard it would be not to get invested in these kids, and her heart sang to think Brandon knew, too, hence his comforting hand. As a teacher, that's what she did — care for her students.

One day at a time. Do not let fear chase me away from Brandon or these children. Lord, help me to seek your will and listen no matter how scary it may seem. Thank you for being with me. You are in front of me, behind me, to the left and right. I can do all things with you in my life.

During one of their breaks, Sarah chatted with other volunteers heading to Kenya for their mission once the orientation was over. They would teach young kids — bound for higher education — to read and write in English. Sarah marveled at the expansiveness of this program.

She wouldn't have minded teaching kids English. She didn't mind this assignment either. Playing every day with kids sounded thrilling. Sarah believed in teaching kids new skills with a preferred skill, like playing. She could teach anything within the parameters of her assignment. It also helped that she'd have the most handsome man in the world on the same field.

"Hey," Brandon startled her from her thoughts. Or maybe she was more shocked at the heat radiating from her shoulder where Brandon's hand rested.

Putting her hand to her chest, "You scared me."

"Sorry. I thought we could grab some lunch before we have to head back for the afternoon session."

Her stomach flip-flopped. If someone had told her that she'd been eating lunch with her ex-fiancé, she would have laughed all the way around her running loop back home. Yet, here she was, in front of him, grabbing a brown bag lunch off the table and a bottle of water. Sometimes, life surprised her.

She'd missed Brandon for the past five years. Back then, guilt and self-consciousness consumed her. Now, she felt confident and ready to have a relationship with Brandon. She didn't know how he felt but needed to clear the air and explain her past actions.

They strolled outside near a Baobab tree. "Is this okay?" Brandon suggested with his hands. Like the gentleman she knew he was, he waited for her to get situated under the tree. Then he sat next to her. He sat so close that the outside of their thighs and shoulders touched, sending ripples down her spine. She wondered if he was affected by their nearness, too.

Sarah ripped open her bag to find a ham and cheese sandwich, an apple, and a chocolate chip cookie. She took a bite of her apple. The silence between them was heavy. Trying to clear up the past would probably tick him off again, so she didn't bother asking right now. "How's your business been?"

"Steady." He took a massive bite of his sandwich.

"My dad says he's been keeping you busy at the store."

"Some, but the house has needed more work than the store." Brandon corrected her.

Taking a deep breath, Sarah slowly let it out. "Are you ready to clear the air?" She'd never been a patient person. Sarah wouldn't spend the next fifteen days avoiding the proverbial elephant in the room.

"I'm enjoying just being. Can we put it off a little longer?" Brandon took another huge bite from his sandwich, leaving him just one more bite. She still hadn't finished her apple.

Come on, Brandon. Sarah bit the inside of her lip to avoid saying anything that she would regret.

"Would you like my sandwich?" Sarah asked, holding it out to him. His eyebrows lifted, questioning her authenticity. "I'm not going to eat it, so if you'd like it, you can have it."

He reached for it. Their fingers brushed against each other, sending a surge of electricity through her arm. She pulled her hand back, clenching her fingers a couple of times.

"Thank you," Brandon smiled.

"I imagine you need more than one sandwich to make muscles like that."

Brandon's appreciative grin spread wide. "You really like how I've grown, don't you?"

Sarah coughed, choking on the bite of the apple she had remaining in her mouth.

Brandon patted her on the back. "You okay?"

The warmth of his hand seeped through her thin tank top. "I'm good."

Insecurity rushed out of her like a river rapid ride out of control. "Brandon, you may need more time to share your thoughts with me, but I need to get this off my chest. "I am sorry for how I ended things — just giving you the ring back and leaving."

She tucked a strand of hair behind her ear, exposing herself on the side closest to Brandon. "No matter what I say, it will not make it better." She hesitated. "I was scared. I didn't think—"

Fardowsa called everyone to return to the classroom, causing Sarah to let out a huff of hair and squeeze her eyes shut.

"Come on. We'll finish this later."

Brandon held out his hand to help her off the ground. When he pulled her up, he used so much force that she slammed into his chest. Her palm heated as it rested on his muscles. They were close enough to kiss. Brandon's eyes dropped to her lips, and the butterflies, already swirling in her stomach, took flight. She wouldn't object to a kiss.

But, instead of kissing her, Brandon stepped back. "Are you okay?" She shook her head, speechless. "I think you lost some weight. You flew up pretty easily."

"Um, thanks, I guess. Rule number one — never tell a woman you've lifted before that she's lost weight. That's something you keep to yourself."

Brandon's runaway chuckle filled the space between them, "Noted." Then he leaned forward, speaking against her cheek, so soft and sweet that his breath moved her hair. "You've always been the perfect size," he said. Goosebumps erupted on her skin, and her spine shuddered.

"Thank you." Sarah felt heat creep up her neck into her face.

"Pink still looks great on you," Brandon teased her about her flushed cheeks.

She bounced her hip off his, which was like a wall. Sarah ricocheted off him. He wrapped his arm around her shoulders to prevent her from falling to the ground. She gazed up at him. His dark chocolate eyes enveloped her. They were again close enough to kiss, but it didn't happen.

She wasn't mad at Fardowsa for interrupting their conversation. Maybe Sarah needed to stop trying to force this. Brandon might not have any more feelings for her, so he didn't want to iron out the past. She grimaced at the thought. The way his eyes held hers told her that wasn't the case, so she just needed to be patient. Perhaps he had so much built-up anger that he feared how it would come out if he started talking. In life, Sarah had tried to follow that quote about taking the most direct way to achieve a goal, yet it left her in the proverbial bushes on the side of the path. When, or if, Brandon wanted to talk about this, he'd have to approach the subject; she wouldn't keep putting herself out there.

"Why did you come to Africa?" Brandon asked Sarah later that evening when they settled into their tent. Tonight, he kept his shirt on; he didn't need to be any more vulnerable than necessary during this conversation. Besides, when Sarah's mouth dropped slightly at the sight of his muscles in this form-fitting shirt, he smirked, liking that he still affected her in that way.

Her body froze.

"Relax. This isn't a trick question." Brandon gently shook her hip.

"I came because Lily asked." Sarah's voice, just barely a whisper.

Brandon chuckled. "Okay, now try it again and be honest."

She whipped onto her back. Shocked, Brandon leaned into the tent, wide-eyed.

"That is the truth. Do you mean to tell me you knew about this little arrangement and came because of this?" Sarah waved her hands around the small tent, almost hitting Brandon in the side of the head.

Brandon captured Sarah's wrist and gently placed her hand on her abdomen. "Settle down, killer. I didn't know you'd be here. I came here to forget about you."

Sarah tried to hide her hurt expression, but he saw it. He didn't want to lie to her, even if it hurt. She liked to hear what he had to say, so she'd have to listen to it all.

Through the years, Brandon had made mental lists of all the things he found attractive about Sarah — that list was long. Besides her silky smooth hair and flawless skin, her toned muscles were at the top. It didn't surprise him, considering how well she ate and all the water she drank, but it added to the many things that led to many sleepless nights.

In addition to her physical features, he fell in love with her heart. He'd never come across a kinder, gentler woman. The only time she didn't exhibit those qualities was when she gave his ring back and only talked to him once they ended up on a plane together bound for Africa.

"I'm ready to hear you out if you're not too tired." Brandon tilted his head, waiting for her answer.

Sarah lowered her gaze, staring at her clasped, hands resting on her stomach. "I felt God was telling me we shouldn't get married. I hated that it would hurt you, but I didn't know what else to do." She let out a big breath.

"Why didn't you tell me?"

Something akin to shame filled her face. Other than a broken heart, silent tension was the worst feeling Brandon had ever experienced. His stomach soured, waiting for her answer.

"Telling the person that you're going to marry that you're still in love with someone else doesn't seem like a great conversation, and I let my fears rule me back then."

Brandon sprang to a seated position, his hands resting on either side of his head and his elbows on his knees. "That sounds like a cop-out," Brandon said accusingly.

"This is why I didn't talk with you five years ago. But if it makes you feel better to yell at me, go ahead."

Brandon ran his hand through his head. "I'm not yelling at you. I'm just frustrated." He looked over his shoulder, not catching her gaze but lowering his voice to a calmer tone. "I just want you to be honest with me." He finally met her eyes. "If I had been good enough, you—"

Sarah cut him off. "—Whoa, hold up. This has nothing to do with you. Guilt tore me apart because I felt like I was betraying Jake by being in love with you, too." Sarah rested her hand on his back. He flinched because he wasn't expecting her soft touch, considering how upset he had made her with her comment. Her cool hand felt like a refreshing lemonade on a hot summer day.

Brandon liked to think he could trust her. But he couldn't help his wandering mind — they wouldn't be in this situation if she had told him this from the beginning.

"I'm sorry I raised my voice at you. I've been thinking this entire time that I wasn't enough for you, or you would have explained why you left. It will take some time to believe otherwise. Let's get some sleep; tomorrow will be a big day."

"You can't stop the conversation when it gets too hard. That's not fair."

"Fair? Says the woman who just admitted that she couldn't converse with me five years ago because she feared what I would say or do. That's rich, Sarah. Some sleep might help you not be a hypocrite. Good night."

As Brandon rolled over to face the tent, he crossed his arms over his chest. Maybe coming to Africa to get closure and move on from Sarah wasn't a great idea after all.

8

On the first day with the kids, Sarah found a spot on the school field with another younger volunteer named Rhys. Many of the younger girls flew around like a kaleidoscope of butterflies. Rhys took the primary-aged girls to use the bathroom, leaving Sarah to chat with the lower-secondary girls.

One minute, these girls shared their hopes and dreams with Sarah, and the next, they watched the boys playing football with Brandon and another male volunteer. Most of their dreams involved getting through school or marrying a Christian boy.

"Did you know that in America, we call that…" she pointed at the boys kicking a ball around. "…soccer. Football is something different."

They ignored Sarah. The way these girls were drooling over the boys, Sarah imagined they would faint if they saw them in a football uniform.

That thought lingered a little too long as she imagined Brandon in football pants. Of course, he caught her staring at him, and when he waved, the girls giggled.

Flirting and attraction must be universal. Although some girls didn't speak fluent English, they were the first to notice the look on my face.

Amina, one of the girls who spoke English fluently, shared what one of the girls said. "Dahabo wants to know if you know either of the hot Americans?" Amina used air quotes around the description of the men.

The man volunteering with Brandon was maybe a decade younger than her and Brandon but still too old for any of these girls. Sarah understood their attraction, though. Both men were built like houses, had smiles that stopped hearts everywhere they traveled, and kindness oozed from their pores. Who wouldn't fall for either of them?

This was going to be a tremendous task — no friend — a mammoth task trying to avoid making a fool of herself with Brandon. The sudden urge to wrap her arms around his strong, firm shoulders, look into his deep brown eyes, and draw him into the most extended, most passionate kiss they'd ever shared filled her entire being.

Amina waved a hand in front of Sarah's face. "Earth to Miss Sarah."

"Oh, sorry." heat filled her face, and it had nothing to do with the seventy-five-degree, dry heat greeting them this early in the morning. "What was the question?"

"Do you know either of them?"

"Yeah. The taller one with brown hair is Brandon." She stopped before revealing more details that would make her sound desperate and pathetic.

Frustrated that she'd let her mind wander to something she knew she shouldn't have, Sarah pulled out a sheet of paper and read the expectations for teaching the kids English. The school provided her with some material, but in Sarah's experience, kids learn so much more if they interact with each other in authentic conversations and games.

At that moment, one of the American soccer balls that the program supplied came barreling toward the group. Dahabo captured the ball, hugging it to her chest. Sarah saw hearts in the girl's eyes when one of the players jogged over and asked for it in Swahili, their native language.

Brandon had told her that all his boys spoke English. Sarah stepped in between their outreached hands. With her eyes on the young man, Sarah asked, "Will you please ask her for the ball in English?"

"Sure." His deep, rugged voice surprised Sarah, yet every girl sighed, making her smile.

Brandon came jogging over. "What's going on?"

"I'm having this young gentleman ask for the ball in English so they can have some authentic practice." Her breath trembled.

Brandon slapped the player on the shoulder. "Adolphe, just ask and get the ball back."

"Dahabo, may I please have the ball?" Adolphe enunciated each word perfectly, clearly having learned English at an early age.

Sarah was too distracted with Brandon a mere foot away. Even so, she had yet to hear Dahabo respond. Instead, she just handed the ball over.

"Thank you," Adolphe grinned.

"This is where you say, 'You're welcome.'" Sarah coached.

"Tank you." Dahabo's broken English made Sarah smile.

As Adolphe took the ball and jogged off with Brandon, Sarah thought she heard Brandon say, "Don't get that look in your eye. Women are trouble. They break your heart." As they put distance between themselves and the girls, Brandon and Adolphe looked back at their respective females.

Heat filled Sarah from the inside out as she held his gaze as long as he'd allow, but her shoulders slumped. She felt like she'd turned Brandon into a pessimist. It didn't help that they still hadn't completely cleared the air yet. Maybe that could be the topic of discussion this evening as they curled up in the cramped tent at sunset.

Despite starting on their own sides last night, Brandon was on his back when they woke up, and Sarah's head rested on his bare chest. Thankfully, she hadn't drooled on him; that would have added to the uncomfortableness of the situation. The contours of Brandon's newly acquired muscles encouraged her to pretend she was sleeping long after she realized Brandon had woken.

The only reason the proximity bothered her was because it clearly bothered Brandon. There was no sense in feeling sad; she'd done this to herself. Right now, they could be happily married and not miles away from each other emotionally and physically, but they weren't, and it was all her doing.

It's a good thing she had these girls to get her back on track. "Way to go, Dahabo." Squeezing the girl's hands, she congratulated her on her English and courage to speak to Adolphe, with whom she was obviously fascinated.

The rest of the day, Sarah and Rhys taught the girls hand games and the team game Red Rover, Red Rover, Come on Over, read Bible stories to them, and talked about the boys with the older girls. Sarah told them they could chat about the boys all day if they wanted. The one condition was that the conversation had to be in English.

The means justified the end for the girls. Amina and Aashka were fluent in English, so every time one of the girls didn't know the English word for what they were trying to say, they asked. The one thing Sarah wouldn't forget ... ever, was her conversation with Dahabo, using her friend, Amina, as a translator. Her heart broke for the young female native. She promised not to say anything, so now she was burdened with keeping the girl's secret.

Through her conversations, Sarah learned that Rhys was married to Jimmy, the volunteer with Brandon. Jimmy was a physical education teacher in the States, and Rhys was a kindergarten teacher. They'd met six years ago when they'd started working at the same school. They married this past summer. Rhys had always wanted to help kids in other countries, so this year, they took a sabbatical to finish their master's degrees with this volunteering opportunity.

"What's the story between you and Brandon?" Rhys encouraged Sarah with a knowing smile.

Sighing too prominently, Sarah silently prayed for the courage to share. "The short story is that we were engaged. I broke it off five years ago this coming December, and this is the first time we've spoken since."

"You're joking?" Rhys and Amina said in unison.

"I wish I were." Sarah confided.

Rhys shook her head, lightly laughing. "I'm no expert, but you two are both hung up on each other. The looks you've been giving each other would need a fire hose to put out the flames. Maybe you two will rekindle things here."

"No chance. He's hurt and angry — which I understand."

"Whatever you say." Rhys stood, releasing all the kids to go home for dinner.

Maybe Rhys was right. Maybe Brandon would let his guard down and accept her apology — he'd have to complete a conversation with her first. Perhaps they could start over again and move on from this misery. Only time will tell.

The day flew by. After cheering on the boys in their game, the girls spent the rest of the day gossiping and giggling about the boys, significantly improving their English.

After the kids left, Brandon, Sarah, Rhys, and Jimmy met back at the host's house, where the medical volunteers were staying, to eat dinner. It was heartwarming how welcoming the natives were toward the volunteers. Tonight, they made coconut bean soup to start. Then they had Wali wa Nazi, rice in coconut milk — to die for — and Mishkaki, beef or chicken kebabs. Sarah hadn't tasted anything so tender and delicious since she'd lived with her dad.

Sarah wasn't sure why she'd moved to Florida. Well, that wasn't entirely true. Selfish motivation to live in a warmer climate and avoid seeing Brandon had driven the car fifteen hundred miles away from her remaining family. If only she could do things over...

As she watched Lily and Kurt dote on each other, getting food for each other, trying each other's drinks, Sarah's soul ached for that intimacy. She'd experienced that yesterday when she gave Brandon her sandwich, but it wasn't the same as sharing food.

The last five years had helped her realize that while she would always have a spot for Jake in her heart, there was more room for Brandon; right now, that level of care she witnessed between Lily and Kurt, she wanted that with Brandon.

Brandon's eyes gazed back at her when she looked up from her plate. She gave him a sheepish smile and dropped her gaze again. Was he reminiscing, too? Sarah wondered if the memories were as painful for Brandon to remember as they were for her.

After dinner, Lily and Kurt shared the events of their day. "We went hiking, and I saw the longest black mamba in Africa..." She paused momentarily before she did what she always does – connect everything to basketball. "...and I don't mean Kobe Bryant. This snake was just about fourteen feet long."

Lily played basketball all through high school and college. Sarah thought her daughter could have made it in the WNBA, but Lily didn't want anything to do with professional sports.

"How do you know how long it was? You weren't that close, were you? Those things are poisonous, you know."

Lily rolled her eyes. Sarah wondered if Lily would continue rolling her eyes into her forties or if the habit would eventually disappear. "Yes, Mom, we know. The guide made sure we were a safe distance away. Don't treat us like babies," said Lily.

Her daughter was annoyed. Lily's comment hadn't bothered Sarah. When Lily had children, she'd know what it felt like to worry about another human being for the rest of her life.

Now and then, Kurt would send Lily alluring eyes. Finally, Sarah hugged her daughter and pushed her toward her husband.

"Good night, you two. We should probably get going before the sun goes down and we get eaten alive. I've been told that those gnats are no joke. They sounded like a swarm of angry bees outside our tent last night."

"I hadn't noticed," Brandon added, studying Sarah's expression.

Sarah and Brandon walked with the happy couple to their room, where she filled her backpack with a change of clothes from her luggage. "Thank you again for storing this." Sarah secured her suitcase. Before she could hoist it to the ground, Brandon stepped in without a word, grabbed the handle, and lifted it like it was nothing. The movement made his biceps bulge, captivating her attention. He set it back on the floor. "T-thank you." Nervous emotion clogged at the back of her throat, forcing her to swallow the hard lump.

"Goodnight. See you tomorrow," Lily said, hugging her mom. Then, she and Brandon left for their tent.

They'd arrived just in time. The gnats were out in full force once they settled into their compact camping accommodations. "I'm glad we're in here and not out there with them." Sarah shivered. Brandon briskly ran his sizeable, calloused hand up and down her arm, creating friction to warm her arms. Electric currents heated her insides.

How'd they even get into this position? She didn't know. Brandon was already lying on his side with his hand supporting his head when she entered the tent after changing.

As soon as she lay down, he surrounded her with his arm like a cocoon. It didn't mean anything. They were working with limited space; he was trying to make them comfortable, that's all.

She was anything but comfortable. Given the proximity, Sarah's heart rate sped out of control. She hadn't been this close to him in years. His intense gaze raised her temperature. If only she were brave enough...her body involuntarily started leaning closer toward his full lips, which she dared to take a sneak at.

Brandon cleared his throat. Sarah jerked back into her space. "I'd love to know what you've been up to – you know, the last five years you've been avoiding me."

Ouch. She had heard the softness in his voice up until the last comment.

He hung his head briefly before his milk chocolate eyes met hers again. "I'm sorry. I shouldn't have said that."

"It's okay. You're right. I moved back to Florida to avoid seeing you. It was too hard. Being here is hard." Sarah squeezed her eyes shut for strength and courage to keep going. "I started teaching online, and I run. That's been my last five years; pretty boring and pathetic."

"Listen, Sarah." Brandon's words came out more like a moan. He tenderly ran his fingers up and down her shoulder and bicep. Even her sweatshirt didn't offer any protection from the tingles invading her body. "If you're pathetic, then so am I because that's what the last five years have looked like for me too. Just add listening to Gus talk about you nonstop, and there you have it."

Sarah laughed. "Yeah, there's that too."

"Are you okay with laying on my chest?"

"Um. I g-guess, if that's more comfortable for you," Sarah stuttered, her heart skipping a beat.

Brandon turned onto his back and dropped his arm around her shoulder. She shifted her body into his side and nestled her head in the crook of his arm. This was such a familiar feeling, yet strange. One would think the added muscle he gained would feel like rocks beneath her head, yet they were a welcome mat for her. Sarah recalled the many nights she'd spent wrapped in this man's arms, cuddling on the couch and watching movies. The warmth of his body used to flow freely from him. But even in this position, Sarah could tell he was guarded and uncomfortable with her.

Sarah didn't have any place to put her right arm. After moving it in three different positions, Brandon gently tugged her wrists toward his chest and placed it on his bare skin. "Is that okay?" His voice, low and rugged.

Sarah sucked in a breath. "Mm-hmm."

"Good night, Sarah." He kissed the top of Sarah's head.

Sarah's breathing slowed as she drifted off to sleep. She hoped this was the beginning of a new start for them.

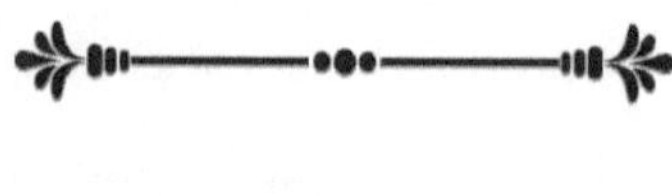

9

Brandon woke up in a sweat. The sun blared on their tent, heating every corner of it. His chest and abs were half covered between Sarah's torso and upper body. Her leg rested on one of his, making Brandon's body feel like an inferno. Heavy eyelids confirmed his lack of sleep. Brandon had been so distracted with Sarah in his arms that he couldn't relax, but he tried. Like old times, Sarah drew circles on his chest to help herself fall asleep. Without fail, she gave in to the sandman quickly while he remained wide awake and breathless. His fingers swelled. Brandon squeezed them into a fist a few times, hoping to regain blood flow.

Sarah's eyes fluttered open. Her limbs stretched out and rolled off him. "I'm so sorry I sprawled all over you."

Are you kidding me? You'd still be there if my stupid arm weren't numb.

"No worries at all. I feel bad for waking you. I was trying to get the feeling back into my arm."

Sarah sat the rest of the way up. "I'm sorry. I should have known better than to sleep on your arm all night."

Brandon rolled up and rested his elbows on his knees. "You have nothing to be sorry for." He kissed her temple. *Where had that come from?* He knew where. The idea of rolling Sarah onto her back and kissing her with abandon had run through his head all night before he fell asleep and then in his dreams some too.

Last night made him realize that no matter how much time passed or how far apart they lived, he would love Sarah for the rest of his life. She had the most irresistible blue eyes and heart-shaped face and lived by the fruits of the spirit. What more could he ask for?

Maybe he could ask for a do-over? He needed to let her know that he still loved her. More than words could say, he adored her. He needed to know if her guilt over Jake had passed and if she still loved him.

Sarah brushed her golden blonde ponytail. He couldn't help but stare; it was longer than he remembered. Brandon had the urge to weave his fingers through the silky waves. Sarah pulled the elastic from the ponytail at the nape of her neck. It was soft and shiny, like a cascade of blonde waters flowing down her back. She continued to run the brush over and under her locks. He had an urge to brush her hair. *What?! Since when has brushing a woman's hair ever been considered the 'thing to do'?*

His resolve was weakening. After five years, he was shocked to see her on the plane. Since then, he'd chained his heart to protect it, but it had been a futile attempt. He couldn't remember a time when he didn't want Sarah in his life.

"Did you sleep okay?" Brandon's voice, soft and concerned.

Sarah pushed onto her knees. "I did, you?"

It was the best night's sleep I'd had in five years. He wouldn't tell her that quite yet. "Yes. Thank you."

Sarah tugged on his arm when they reached the volunteer's house for breakfast and blurted out, "I was scared."

Confusion ran through Brandon. "Scared about what?"

Sarah felt her resolve crumbling. "That I'd dishonor Jake." He searched her eyes. "I felt so guilty about loving and marrying you that I couldn't take it."

"Oh, Sweetheart, come here." Brandon wrapped his arms around her shoulders, and she rested her arms around his waist. She placed the side of her face on his chest. It didn't take long for him to feel the moisture on his shirt. Her shoulders shook gently. He pulled her back just enough to look into her piercing blue eyes. "Don't worry about that now." Using the pads of his thumbs, he wiped her tears.

How could he be angry with her when she cried? Even though he knew women could break a man's resolve, he'd never experienced this until he met Sarah; she captured his heart.

"We have to worry about it, or we won't grow." Sarah shuddered out.

"Is that what you want? To grow?" Brandon studied her.

The door flung open before Sarah could answer him. "Mom, how was your first day?" Lily grabbed her mom's arm and dragged her inside.

Sarah looked back at Brandon. He thought her eyes said, *I wish we could still talk,* but she was gone.

He couldn't believe that her guilt ran so deep that she thought it had been best to call off the wedding. *I would have waited and helped her get through those feelings. Why hadn't she trusted me enough?*

Today, Brandon taught the boys how to play basketball even though football, AKA soccer, was their preferred sport. As he handed out the orange pinnies to one team, he spied Sarah, teaching the girls some cheers in English. Thankfully, no one was watching because his eyes swept over her length. She could make a simple tank top and jean shorts look elegant. He wondered if Sarah would bring the girls to the court to cheer for the boys. The thought frustrated him. He wasn't supposed to be fantasizing about

Sarah. The purpose of this trip was to get closure. Yet, all this trip had done was remind him how great Sarah was.

Jimmy gathered the boys to teach them the proper form for a layup. They ran a layup drill on the right side, then the left. After that, Brandon showed the boys free throws.

"Take your time. It's just you and the basket. Stabilize yourself. Bend your knees slightly, bring the ball to eye level, and place your palm like this." Brandon showed the boys his fingers spread slightly. "Tuck your elbow into your side. Your guide hand should not bear weight on the ball; it's meant to keep it in your palm. When you're ready to shoot, push from the shoulder, extend through the elbow, and flick your wrist. Your fingertips will roll off the ball, and all four fingers will point downward when the ball releases." Swoosh.

Brandon stepped out of the way as Jimmy retrieved the ball. "Boys, line up one behind the other and practice your free throws."

While the boys shot, Jimmy and Brandon encouraged them and fixed their form when necessary. "Rhys and I are climbing part of Mt. Kilimanjaro this weekend if you and Sarah want to join us."

"Thanks, man, but Sarah wants to do that with her daughter and son-in-law. We're hoping to do it before we leave. But I need to find something to wow her this weekend."

Jimmy smirked. "So Rhys was right. You still love her. According to her, Sarah loves the water. Why don't you take her to Victoria Falls? It's one of the seven wonders of the world."

There wasn't any point in denying his love for her. Brandon had texted Gus earlier this morning, and he'd also reminded Brandon about Sarah's fascination with water. He took that as a sign to plan something near water, but it had to be unique, an experience she couldn't get at home.

"That would be great! Have you been?"

"Yeah, our last mission was in Zimbabwe. It's something you don't want to miss." Jimmy assured him.

"Keep your elbow in Adolphe," Brandon called out.

"Zimbabwe? How long of a flight is that?" Brandon wondered aloud.

"Eleven hours. But I have a buddy you could stay with and then fly back for Monday."

Brandon's jaw dropped. "That's not a weekend trip." Most New Englanders don't want to travel more than thirty minutes for dinner, so an eleven-hour flight was a complete vacation to him.

The girls arrived on the court. Rhys sidled up to Jimmy, wrapping her arm around his lower back. Brandon looked longingly at Sarah, wishing that was them.

"Hey." her soft voice penetrated through his chest. His heart threatened to explode. Staying upset with her wasn't an option. His heart swelled with joy every time Sarah came around.

"Hey. Did you bring the girls to cheer for the boys?" He asked as she passed him to speak with one of the girls.

"Maybe." Sarah's sweet smile elevated his heartbeat even more.

Brandon watched Sarah with Dahabo. She seemed like a nice girl. Adolphe confided in Brandon that he liked her. If he knew Sarah, her brain was working overtime to bring the two teens together, if that was possible. It looked like a heavy conversation; he'd ask Sarah about that later.

Besides, when they were in the tent, it was rare that Brandon and Sarah were alone, so when he noticed the blonde beauty standing solo on the field, he moved closer, letting their shoulders touch. He said a silent prayer for strength and courage. Then he crossed his arms over his chest and declared, "I'd like to surprise you with a fun getaway this weekend if you're up for it." He had faith that something would come to mind.

Her eyes studied his. If she kept looking at him like that, he'd have no choice but to kiss her. Brandon let out a little growl when she pulled the corner of her bottom lip between her teeth. "Just let me know." He jetted off to the other side of the court with Jimmy before he captured her lips right there in front of all these kids.

Brandon and Jimmy separated the boys by age and then divided each group in half for the games. *Hopefully, the boys remembered the rules and didn't get distracted by the girls cheering for them.* Heck, Brandon hoped he didn't get distracted watching Sarah instruct the girls.

Meanwhile, Rhys and Sarah did the same with the girls. Rhys took the younger girls to cheer for the boys their age, and Sarah kept the older girls who would cheer for the boys with Brandon. It'd taken most of the day for some of the girls to get the English translations correct, but their determination and drive to do this activity kept them going strong. With Sarah, Rhys, Amina, and Aashka, the four of them could divide and conquer.

Rhys and Jimmy did such an excellent job with the younger kids. The boys traveled from one end of the court to the other, and the girls fluttered around like butterflies half the time, but they had fun.

On the other hand, Brandon had so much pent-up energy that he appreciated Sarah's reminder to relax after he barked out directions while the boys played their game. *Relax, ha! How could he relax with Sarah mere inches away from him? Was her guilt the only reason she'd left, or was there more?* Brandon had spent the better part of the last five years believing that he wasn't good enough for her. Those scars ran deep. How was he going to get past the hurt?

"The kids are having a blast and learning a lot." Sarah reasoned.

"How could they not when they have the best teacher." Brandon pointed toward the boys playing ball.

Sarah chuckled. "That's so nice of you to consider me the best. I mean, look at Dahabo." She gently bumped shoulders with him. He looked down at her full lips and then back to her eyes. They burst out in laughter. He'd missed this — her teasing and laughing at his fake ego.

"What are you so worked up about?" Sarah's nearness threatened to send him over the edge. He considered himself a strong man, but he was a man nonetheless. The electric tension between them made his pulse race.

He agreed that Dahabo had made the most progress with her English in the last few days, just as Adolphe had grown the most in his athleticism. Based on Brandon's conversations with the young man, he knew the high schooler had harbored a crush on the girl since they were in middle school, but his dad wouldn't let him date any girl who didn't speak fluent English, claiming an English-speaking woman was Adolphe's ticket to a successful life.

Sarah had shared how determined Dahabo was to learn the language, and he wondered if she carried feelings around for Adolphe. Now, with her English improving, maybe they could finally be together. Brandon had grown fond of the teen and wanted the best for him.

Suddenly, Dahabo collapsed to her knees. Sarah, Brandon, Amina, and Adolphe were at her side, assaulting her with questions. Her eyes moved back and forth like ping-pong balls among the crew. Amina silenced everyone and spoke to Dahabo in Swahili before reporting, "She said she's fine. Just needs some water."

"Are you sure?" Adolphe questioned her with concerned, hard eyes. She nodded, her eyes soft and assuring.

Brandon found that interesting. Although he wasn't always the most observant man, he wondered if something was already happening between the two teens.

When their time ended for the day, the kids walked home, Jimmy and Rhys drove to their host's home, and Brandon and Sarah walked to their camping area. He intentionally walked close to her, grazing her shoulder. He felt like a shy teenager walking his girlfriend home from school, praying he'd be brave enough to hold her hand.

"Dahabo and Adolphe will make a sweet couple someday. It's clear they both like each other." The excitement in Sarah's voice made Brandon smile.

The urge to lace his fingers with hers persisted, but he resisted. Sarah still hadn't agreed to a little getaway, so he didn't want to press his luck. Instead, he bumped her shoulder again.

"You are great with those girls. They hang onto your every word and do everything you ask of them."

"Thanks for the compliment, but I don't think it's me. They're great with Rhys, too. We just found their interest and capitalized on it, and it just so happens their interest is in your boys."

Brandon laughed. "My boys have the same interest. The boys aren't allowed to date any girl who isn't fluent in English."

"Ah. That explains Dahabo's motivation. Imagine being Amina or Aashka. They must get pestered for dates all the time."

"Maybe," Brandon said as he walked backward, locking Sarah with his gaze. "Or maybe boys like Adolphe are waiting for girls like Dahabo to figure things out so he can be with the one he wants."

Brandon knew that Sarah understood the analogy by the look in her eyes. "That's a sweet thought, but how long before he gives up and moves on if it takes her longer than one would anticipate to *figure things out*?"

"If he truly loves her, he'll never move on," Brandon deadpanned. Without thinking, he stopped, and Sarah stepped into his space, closing the gap between them. His desire to press his lips to hers consumed him, and he searched her eyes for a sign.

"Brandon," Sarah whispered.

He loved how his name sounded on her lips. Was it too soon to kiss her again?

She took a step back and to the side. He jogged to catch up with her. "I'd love to get away with you this weekend." Sarah bumped gently against his shoulder.

"Awesome," Brandon spoke, overwhelmed by her inner and outer beauty. Maybe this trip was all they needed to move on together.

10

"How did everyone's day go?" Sarah asked at the host's table but couldn't wait to hear from Lily and Kurt.

"Kurt and I could only travel to one local school to administer immunizations to kids who were behind on their shots or haven't had any to date." Lily took a bite of her ugali, which Sarah could only describe the flour mixture like America's mashed potatoes, sort of.

These schools were about thirty minutes from where Sarah and Brandon were volunteering. They had been invaded by tribal groups trying to recruit new blood.

"Hopefully, the trouble will go away, and we can finish the immunizations tomorrow."

"Yeah. The kids were so appreciative. They hugged us and made us pictures. It's so nice to make a difference," Kurt added.

The liveliness at the table spoke volumes. Sarah had become fast friends with the other volunteers. She couldn't believe she'd almost missed out on this experience. *Thank you, Lord, for helping me wake up and do good for others instead of sulking in self-pity. Thank you for bringing Brandon back into my life. If it be your will, help me keep him in my life.*

"What did you do the rest of the day?"

"We went to Nairobi National Park and are now fostering an elephant with the Wildlife Trust. It's so sad, Mom. An elephant is killed for its ivory every fifteen minutes. The poaching here isn't as bad as in China and Thailand, but it's bad enough."

Sarah listened to her daughter, and she could hear the love and care she had for God's creatures. Sarah knew Lily was out doing good in the world, and she couldn't have been more proud. "Lily, you are one of a kind, you know that."

Lily laughed before telling her mom about the safari ride they had gone on. "We saw the Big Five."

When Sarah looked confused about the Big Five, Kurt explained. "You know, lion, leopard, rhino, elephant, and buffalo. The hunters call them the Big Five here in Africa because they are the most difficult animals to shoot and have the most relentless personalities when being hunted. Therefore, they are the most widely desired to be seen."

Sarah's ringtone jolted from the conversation. Gus's face filled the screen. "It's my dad. I'll be right back." Sarah whispered to Brandon before she excused herself.

"Hi, Dad. How are you?"

"I'm still living the dream. How about you? How's Africa?" Gus's voice was sly and full of wonder.

Sarah chuckled. "You were in on this little setup, weren't you? Lemme guess, you are the mastermind who made Lily and Kurt be your henchmen."

"I'm glad you're not mad. It's nice to hear you laugh again." Sarah smiled, knowing her dad did this for her — to make her happy — not to upset her.

"Thanks for always being there, Dad. I've been thinking. . . when I leave here, would it be okay to put my home up for sale and come live with you for good this time?"

"Does this mean you and Brandon are back together?"

"No, Dad, it doesn't. It just means I realized I shouldn't miss time with you."

"Of course, you can come live here. This is your home. How are things going with you and Brandon?"

"We've been spending a lot of time together, so we'll see what happens. I'm not making any promises. I really hurt him, Dad." Sarah put her free hand to her forehead as she turned around to find Brandon standing right behind her. Heat rose to her cheeks.

"Um, Dad, I have to go, but I'll call you on Monday with finalized plans. I love you."

"He's right there, isn't he?" Gus's excitement didn't go unnoticed.

"Yes, Dad, he is." Sarah blushed.

"Good. Tell him I said, 'Hi'." Sarah did as her Dad asked.

Brandon got closer than necessary and hollered into the phone, "Hey, Gus."

"You're taking care of my girls, right?" Gus demanded.

"Yes, Sir. I'm keeping a close eye on Sarah. Kurt's doing his husbandly duty as well," Brandon assured the older gentleman.

"I love you, Sarah. I'm glad you're having revelations on this trip. See you soon. Bye, Brandon."

"Love you too. Bye, Dad."

Brandon shoved his hands in his pockets. "Sorry, I didn't mean to intrude, but we should gather your stuff from Lily and Kurt's room and get moving before we regret it."

Embarrassment filled Sarah's body. How much had he heard? She spoke the truth, and it wasn't anything Brandon didn't already know, but admitting it out loud still made her feel awful.

"For what it's worth, what appears as madness is just sadness. Like you said, you hurt me, Sarah." Brandon placed his hand on the small of her back as he led her into the house behind Lily.

His hot breath on her neck produced goosebumps on her skin. "Hopefully, we're moving past the hurt and into a future where we can let our guards down."

It was another close call getting back to their tent before the gnats feasted on them for the evening. Sarah had anticipated how the evening would end. She'd find Brandon in shorts, bare-chested, lying in his spot in the tent. Her pulse would race and eventually settle a long time after she'd positioned herself next to him in her spot. This is how the other nights had concluded, not that she was complaining.

Tonight was different, though — not in activity but in feeling. Sarah felt like Brandon was slowly coming around. She hoped he'd forgive her soon. One thing was for sure — her feelings for Brandon had intensified. So, when she found him as expected, Sarah wanted more than just going to sleep. She needed to finish their talk in order to move on.

Instead of lying down, Sarah sat next to him, resting her forearms on her knees. "Can we talk?"

Brandon propped himself up on his elbow. "Sure."

Sarah didn't waste any time. "What are we doing here?"

"What do you mean?" Brandon rubbed the back of his neck.

Sarah ran her hands on the front of her pajama pants and bit her lip. "We're forced to stay in this tent, but nobody is forcing you to flirt with me."

"Me?! What about you?" Brandon choked out. "First, I'm not good enough for you. Now, you act like we haven't been apart for the past five years." She'd never heard his voice so brass before, at least not toward her.

Sarah jerked her head toward him, capturing Brandon's forlorn features with her eyes. "You're more than enough. This had nothing to do with you. I told you I couldn't get over my guilt around Jake. It had too much of my headspace and ripped me away from you."

"I wish you would have talked to me. We could have worked through it together; we didn't have to cut each other off. How am I supposed to trust you?"

This conversation was going differently than she'd planned. How could she show him that she cared about him? What would she have to do for him to trust her? The silence in the tent got on her nerves.

Sarah groaned as she plopped back in her spot, resting the back of her hand on her forehead. "I feel even worse because you thought you weren't good enough — that was never the case." What had she done? Would she be able to fix this? God willing, yes!

"I need a drink," Brandon said out of the blue.

He'd never drank before. His pain must have gotten so bad that he'd given in to temptation. "Since when do you drink?"

"Since right now."

"That's not funny. We can get through this if you let me back in — I can help you."

Brandon lay on his side, propped up on his elbow. "I'm a big boy; I'll be okay. Besides, you've *helped me enough*."

Sarah hadn't expected him to be so grumpy about this. She didn't expect him to let her jump right back into his arms, but she hoped he wouldn't say rude comments under his breath like the one he mumbled when he was on the field with Adolphe getting the ball from Dahabo. Nor did she expect him to be grumpy with her when she opened her heart to him. His hot and cold demeanor was getting on her nerves. If he's going to be mad, then be mad, but his eyes and hand on her back were doing enough flirting on their own to send mixed messages.

She playfully squeezed his bicep. "Yes, you are a big boy." Sarah winked at him, trying to get him to relax.

"Quit flirting with me. How am I ever supposed to keep my guard up if you touch me and say things like that?"

"You could always let the walls crumble, and we can rebuild them together."

Brandon ran his hand through his hair and gripped the back of his neck. "Where does this leave us now?" he asked as if he had yet to reach a conclusion. He leaned closer. Was he going to kiss her? Brandon shifted his body toward her. She saw it — a glimpse of the Brandon she knew five years ago before she walked away, the one who loved her. Is it possible that he longed to rekindle their relationship just as much as she desired?

Her heart beat a few times as his intense gaze threatened to devour her right here, right now. "I know that I've worked through my guilt, and I've never stopped loving you," she whispered as he grew closer.

"Sarah?" Brandon's deep voice moved closer to her ear.

"Hmm," she couldn't speak.

"I've never stopped loving you either. I won't lie — I'm scared. Five years ago, I thought we'd get married and live happily ever after. Then, you pulled the rug out from underneath me. The thought of that happening again makes me want to puke."

Sarah loved this man even more. Most men wouldn't reveal such raw emotion. Running the palm of her hand over his face, she gently guided him toward her; she couldn't think of anything she wanted more than to feel Brandon's lips on hers again.

Before that could happen, Brandon yanked himself away from her hand. "Sarah, I need more time." He crossed his arms over his chest. "Get some rest. We'll need energy for tomorrow. Good night, Sarah."

"Okay." All the air deflated from Sarah's lungs as she turned her back to Brandon. "Good night, Brandon."

Squeezing her eyes as tight as humanly possible, she couldn't stop the tears that began to escape from the corners of her eyes.

The night crept by slowly. Sarah couldn't even fall asleep by concentrating on Brandon's steady breathing. Desperately, she prayed that God's will be done and for strength and courage for both of them since it seemed like someone would still be broken after this trip.

Brandon spent a lonely, miserable night hugging himself. His arms screamed in rebellion; they wanted to be wrapped around Sarah. Was he being petty or selfish? He hoped not. He trusted Sarah in general but didn't trust her with his heart — not yet, not anymore.

She looked angelic as she slept. Her flawless skin was smooth and bright. He swallowed, trying to moisten his dry throat. All he could think about at that moment was running his fingers through her silky, blonde locks.

He felt like a jerk. Sarah had finally returned to him, guilt-free and able to love him, yet he'd been cross with her. He needed to burn off this energy before he did or said anything else he'd regret.

He unzipped and rezipped the tent as quickly as possible, trying not to disturb Sarah's slumber. Thankfully, Kyle agreed to join him on a guided trail run. He couldn't wait to see to see Mount Kilimanjaro. According to the company, experienced guides create a custom route for their customers.

They only had two hours before their day began, so their route would only cover the lower elevation of the mountain, but that would be good enough for now.

Kyle exited the house like a church mouse. When he reached Brandon about five feet away, he slapped him on the back. "Ready to go, Man?"

"Definitely."

The ride to Moshi Town was quiet this early in the morning. The natives were starting to stir. Brandon appreciated how hard they worked from sun-up to sundown. He hated the difficulties they faced with lack of water, sanitation, and enemies. Any of those things by themselves would be enough to deal with, but all three at once — that's rough. Even if things with Sarah didn't get resolved during this trip, coming here was the best decision he'd made in his life.

"Something bothering you today?" Kyle asked.

Brandon continued to stare out the window. "Sarah said that she's over the guilt she had before and ready to love me."

"That's great. Why do you look like your dog just died then?"

"What if she's still not ready?" Brandon ran his palms on his thighs. "The last five years did a job on me, Kyle. I can't have her pull away from me again."

"I get it, but you must either forgive her and move on or let her know you can't."

He knew Kyle spoke the truth. If things were going to be different between him and Sarah, Brandon would have to put his heart out there again. Were there things she was still keeping from him that would creep in later, or had she laid all her feelings out at this point?

Brandon felt his shoulders relax as they exited the car at their destination. Their guide warmed them up and started on the trail he'd mapped out for them. The clear air helped him decide that Sarah was worth the risk of another broken heart. He hoped he didn't regret this decision.

11

It had been almost a week since he had consciously decided to let Sarah back in, but sadly, he hadn't seen an opportunity to share that information with her. They had been working all the time, and when they weren't with the students, they were sightseeing with the other volunteers. Besides, he'd spent the majority of his time praying – his heart said, "Move on, tell Sarah you love her." His head was another story. "You'll get hurt again. How do you know she's ready? Don't be a fool." He wasn't a fan of his head's messages, but he had a hard time ignoring them, too.

"I'm sorry." Sarah brushed up against his shoulder on their most recent walking tour that Adolphe suggested.

He lightly bumped her with his shoulder. "Nothing to be sorry for." When his shoulder bumped her delicate arm, it warmed him instantly. Tenderly as ever, Sarah ran her fingertips down his forearm and briefly laced her fingers with his. Then she stopped at an outdoor market and searched for a new bracelet for Lily.

To his dismay, they hadn't reconnected for the rest of the tour. Given his on-and-off grumpy attitude toward her lately, he was surprised that Sarah had shown him any affection. Her gentleness spoke volumes about her character, emphasizing one of the many reasons he was drawn to her.

By the time they'd reached the tent last night, he had planned to ask her if she was sure she could give her heart to him. Instead, she accused him of hating her.

"You would have hated me even more if I had married you before. I wouldn't have been the wife you needed. But I guess it doesn't matter. You hate me now anyway, so I didn't stand a chance either way."

He didn't hate her. He thought he did once, but that had been the pain and hurt tearing through his body like a tsunami destroying everything in its path, making him believe he hated her.

People don't get mad unless they care. *Care*? That didn't even scratch the surface of his feelings for Sarah. This woman was his whole life. He flew to another continent, trying to get over her. Instead, God led them together on this single mission to a single tent.

Tonight didn't go much better. When they arrived "home" — he used that term loosely — she hadn't been rude but hadn't listened to him either. Instead, she expressed that she was too exhausted to talk, rolled over, and drifted off to sleep. He knew her better than she thought. Sarah obviously felt rejected the other night, and maybe tonight, too, when he didn't initiate hand-holding after she bought Lily's jewelry.

Brandon had spent another restless night trying to figure out how to apologize for his moodiness and tell her he was ready to give their relationship another chance. He never intended to be cranky with her; it just happened when he let her know how he felt. In the wee hours of the morning, he thought he'd finally created a game plan for protecting their hearts. His heavy lids finally surrendered to the sandman.

The sun scorched through their tent. He rolled over, expecting to share his idea with Sarah, but she wasn't there.

"Sarah?" His questioning tone filled the tent.

Nothing. Where could she have gone? The only explanation he had was breakfast. That's right. She must be at the volunteer's house eating with the others. *Didn't she remember the danger she put herself in by being out and about alone?* Besides, they'd been going to meals together, but after the difficult moments they'd had the last couple of nights, he should have expected Sarah to pull away. Maybe his head was right? She wouldn't be able to handle his raw emotions and end up leaving him again. Conceivably, it was a good thing he hadn't said anything to her yet.

Brandon dressed and rushed to breakfast, hoping to clear the air before he and Sarah started their day. Skipping over every pothole in the rutted dirt road, Brandon prayed God watched out for him. All he needed was to twist an ankle or worse. The intense humidity had already soaked through Brandon's shirt before the sun could peek beyond the horizon. Finally, the host's house came into view. He picked up his pace.

Scanning the room, Brandon started to panic when he didn't see Sarah. *Come on, Sarah, where are you?* He could have kicked himself. His need for more time didn't matter any longer. All he needed to do was find Sarah. If she were here, he'd explain that he only needed more time to ensure that proximity wasn't the only reason she shared her feelings. Another truth — being so close to Sarah was playing with his mind. The thoughts swirling in his head needed to be shut down before he crossed lines that he shouldn't.

"Good Morning." The Tanzanian host greeted Brandon.

Forcing a smile to hide his near-panic state, Brandon responded automatically. "Good morning. Thank you again for your hospitality."

"Where's the wife this morning?" The man spoke fluent English, but Brandon needed a few extra seconds to process the man's question.

"Oh, no. Sarah's not my wife. She—'

"—why not?" the host interrupted.

Pain pierced Brandon's chest. He didn't have time to explain the last five years to this generous man; he needed to find Sarah. How pathetic he would sound if he revealed how Sarah retracted her desire to marry him, yet here they were, still single and forced to share a tent.

"It's a long story. Maybe there'll be time to share some time. Excuse me." Though he felt terrible, Brandon didn't wait for the man's response when he spied Lily.

"Hey. Have you seen your mom?"

Looking around the room, Lily lifted one shoulder and let it fall. "Not this morning. Why? Isn't she with you?"

"No. I told her last that I still … it doesn't matter. I'm heading to school. If she's not there, I'll text you."

"You told her what? Are you two getting back together?" Excitement zipped through Lily's voice.

Shrugging his shoulders, Brandon raced out the door. Fear started to consume Brandon. Not only was he worried about Sarah being in physical danger, given the attacks continuing to happen against native Christians and missionaries alike, but his concern grew for her being in a foreign country, unsure of how to get anywhere. Brandon silently chuckled, thinking of Sarah's inability to get to an unknown location without the GPS on her phone. Lily shared a family joke with him years ago. When she was earning a navigation badge for Girl Scouts, her mom got them lost. Fortunately, Lily said her dad was a pro. The next time she tried to earn the badge, she brought her dad and earned it easily. Hopefully, her navigation skills had improved.

As he rushed to the school, he prayed. *Lord, please let Sarah be okay physically and emotionally. Things don't operate the same way here as in the States.* Brandon knew what happened to many native women, especially if they were found alone. He picked up his pace as the dreadful thought of anything happening to Sarah now crossed his mind. *Once I find her, help me clearly explain my feelings so she understands. Open her heart and her mind to our potential future.*

By the time Brandon reached the school, sweat had rolled down his neck and back as the sun waged war on his skin. Scanning the field, he saw the majority of the group in the same close vicinity — the boys with Jimmy and the girls with Rhys. *Where are you, Sarah?*

His cell phone rang. It only took him half a ring to answer his phone. "Hello," he answered in a rush.

"Did you find her?" Lily blared into the phone.

Brandon spun around like he was trying to conceal his conversation, but from whom? He was in the middle of the school field, with the closest group of people being thirty feet away from him. "No."

He was bound to find her before he did anything else this morning. He spun back around to scan the area again. Beyond the group, far in the distance, he saw two figures walking toward the rest of the crew. "I found her, Lily."

"Let her know I don't appreciate being scared like that."

Brandon swallowed the chuckle that tried to escape. "Trust me, I'll let her know."

For just a moment after disconnecting the call, Brandon thanked the good Lord for keeping Sarah safe. Then, he hightailed it in her direction. Once he reached her and quickly greeted her, he sidled up to Sarah, gently grabbing her elbow. "Can I have a word with you, please?"

"We need to get going on our field trip." Sarah tried to dismiss him.

Brandon pulled her aside, saying, "It can wait."

He tugged her a little too hard, and she stumbled over her feet. Brandon steadied her with both of his hands on her arms. "Sorry." He crossed his arms over his chest and spread his legs wider than hip-width to be eye-level with her. "Care to tell me why you disappeared this morning?"

Sarah's eyes widened, and she mimicked his stature with her arms crossed over her chest. "Disappeared?"

"Don't play coy with me. We always ate together and walked to school together. You know that you're a target for the tribal gangs or a potential martyr for the Islamic groups. You put your life in jeopardy. Why'd you leave without me?"

She let her arms fall to her sides. "I didn't disappear. Actually, I had a hunch that something was wrong with Dahabo, so I left when God nudged me to check on her."

He hated looking like an idiot. Of course, she wouldn't do something dangerous to spite him. Sarah had always been forthcoming with him; why did he think she'd change now? Her obedience to help a child sounded precisely like Sarah.

"It just so happens that God's call coincided with your request for time and space," Sarah's voice oozed with sweet sarcasm.

Brandon looked away from her, ran his hands through his hair, and brought his legs closer together, making him reach his full height. "Sarah, I didn't mean to hurt you. When I woke up this morning, I wanted to explain what I meant—"

Sarah put her hand up to stop his words. "Please, don't make this any harder than it has to be. I get it. I messed up years ago and then again by not attempting to fix it before now. I have to live with that. However, we're both adults. We can manage to co-exist. We must share a tent and teach at the same school for the next few days. I'm sorry I made it more difficult on you." She turned to walk away.

Oh no. Walking away again wasn't an option. He couldn't bear the thought of Sarah slipping away from him again. He was willing to yell, scream, and fight with this woman, but under no circumstance would this be the end.

Brandon gently pulled her back to him so her arm pressed firmly against his chest. Her wildberry perfume attacked his senses, causing him to steady his breath before speaking. His lips grazed the side of her head while he whispered, "I needed more time — a break — so I didn't act on my selfish thoughts."

He felt Sarah's body stiffen. Small bumps grew on her arm underneath Brandon's hand. "Oh," Sarah shivered. "I just assumed ... I'm sorry."

She continued to stare straight ahead, but he didn't care. If their eyes connected right now, like those of a hormonal teenager, he wouldn't be able to keep his lips off her. "Please don't take off without telling someone where you're going," Brandon continued to whisper into her hair. "We'll finish this conversation tonight." He pressed a lingering kiss to her temple before returning to the group. "It's time to go."

One moment at a time, Brandon repeated to himself. He felt Sarah's shift and saw her intense look when he shared his weakness — her. Now, she understood exactly what he meant when he told her he needed space. When they settled down for the night, they would discuss their future.

Brandon cleared his throat. "Are you guys ready?" Brandon fist-bumped Jimmy, Adolphe, and the rest of the boys.

"Yeah!" the kids roared collectively.

Sarah finally joined the group. Given his proximity to Sarah, Brandon's body temperature had risen. The proximity also had Brandon's heart racing out of control, and he didn't know when it would recede. His core bubbled like magma as her alluring eyes studied him. Her slightly flushed cheeks told him all he needed to know.

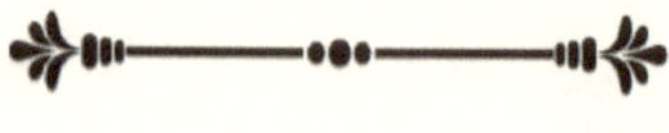

12

Selfish thoughts! Brandon had blindsided her with his comments. What was she supposed to do with them? She'd like to kiss him, but she wouldn't. He needed to make the first move. The last thing Sarah wanted to do was push him into something before his heart was ready for it. He needed to be more clear. One minute, he'd told Sarah that he needed space, leading her to believe that maybe being together all the time smothered him. Then, the next minute, his muscles and deep, raspy voice told Sarah he wanted more. Good grief.

The tour guide leading them to the hot springs scared Sarah. Not in a creeper sort of way, but in a *do you actually have a license to drive this thing* kind of way? She understood the road would be rough with bumps and potholes. But did he have to drive a hundred miles per hour over them? Apparently. He sped over Every. Single. One.

Bumping into Brandon, she grabbed his leg. Her palm rested on his muscular thigh, causing her breath to still briefly. He wrapped his firm, muscular arm around her shoulders. Having Brandon's arm around her was one benefit of the man's poor driving skills. Fortunately, the road evened out thirty minutes into the trek. Unfortunately, Brandon removed his arm to check on the kids behind them, and he'd never put it back. He hadn't attempted to hold her hand while exploring with the other volunteers either. She had to accept the fact that he must have moved on since she knew his love language was touch, and he wasn't doing much of that.

She and Brandon couldn't talk about their relationship right now, so she let her mind focus on Dahabo. Watching her and Adolphe sit snuggled in the seat warmed her heart. They looked so happy, but how long would that happiness last? Having to live by such constringent expectations and rules would drive Sarah crazy. She hoped that in the next few days, the teens could create a plan that their parents couldn't ignore. What would become of her situation if Dahabo didn't become fluent in English?

"Sarah." She heard a voice, she thought was Amina's, holler from the back of the bus where Rhys and Jimmy were sitting.

Turning toward the voice, Sarah's guess proved correct. Amina had a massive smirk on her face. "Rhys and Jimmy taught us a chant. Want to hear it?"

Without kneeing Brandon in the back, she twisted her leg around so her calf was perpendicular to the seat. "Go for it."

"Ready girls?" Amina started them off. "Sarah and Brandon up in a tree. K-I-S-S-I-N-G..."

Sarah's mouth dropped as the chant continued. Heat rose up her neck and settled over her face. Can you say embarrassing? At least Brandon wasn't looking at her. What was he thinking? Would he think they sat around and talked about him all day? Maybe. She did tell them that the girls liked to talk about the boys, and as long as they spoke in English, that was fine. She'd indeed thank Jimmy and Rhys for the girl's extra lesson later.

When the chant finished, Sarah clapped. "Nice English girls. I'm super proud of you." Then she turned back around, hoping to seem calm about the whole charade.

Brandon turned back into the seat. He gently bounced his elbow off her shoulder. "Nice try, but your red cheeks reveal your embarrassment."

"Ah, that's where you're wrong. I don't get embarrassed. I might be shocked but not embarrassed. I think what you witnessed was shock and worry all in one."

"Worry?" Brandon quirked an eyebrow at her.

Sarah ducked her chin and wrapped a tendril of escaped hair from her ponytail around her ear. Brandon lifted his forefinger under her chin until her eyes met his. "I thought you'd be bothered by the chant."

"Bothered as in upset or hot and bothered?" Brandon winked at her.

Interestingly enough, Brandon seemed to be his calm, teasing self. On the other hand, Sarah let his musky scent cloud her self-control. "If they want to see kissing, perhaps we should give it to them." A gentle suggestion never hurt. Some men took way too long to figure things out. That's comical coming from Sarah. This man had hung on to her for years.

The words were suspended in mid-air. He didn't respond to them, and Sarah couldn't pull them back into her mouth and nestle them safely in her brain like they never escaped. She felt like an idiot. What happened to let him make a move? She bumped his shoulder. "Don't look so scared. I'm totally kidding."

To avoid further embarrassment, Sarah gazed out her window. What was she thinking? Obviously, Brandon was just teasing her. Oh, how she loved that. If she could only pick one thing she missed about him the most, it would be his flirtatious teasing. The way he used to drop innuendos or tease her about being short. She loved everything about Brandon.

Finally, they reached Kikuletwa Hot Spring. The younger kids skipped ahead of everyone, eager to use the Tarzan swing. The tour guide led the group past the picnic tables, which they would use later for a lunch break.

Surrounded by trees, Sarah felt like a caterpillar wrapped in a chrysalis awaiting transformation. She knew hot potting was a concern, but right now, Sarah wanted to soak in the hot spring until she melted away. Brandon hopped off the bus the second it stopped, making it clear that he couldn't wait another moment to put some distance between the two of them for one reason or another.

Jimmy and Rhys took the kids who wanted to jump in the turquoise-colored lagoon to the Tarzan swing, where the depth of the water made it safe. Sarah figured Brandon tagged along with them since she hadn't seen him since they'd arrived. Dahabo, Amina, and Aashka entered the lagoon using the wooden ladder with Sarah.

As soon as Sarah set her feet on the ladder, little fish started nibbling at them. She shook one foot at a time, trying to deter the creatures, but it didn't work.

"You need to start moving, and they'll leave you alone," Amina said, her voice soft and giggling.

Sarah listened. The next challenge was the current. Multiple ropes were attached to tree roots for guests to grab if they wanted to soak in the spring. Otherwise, the current would send them drifting down the lagoon.

"Are you doing okay, Dahabo?" Sarah's voice was concerned.

The young girl shook her head as she grabbed a rope to avoid the current pushing her downstream.

Amina and Aashka joined the duo. "Sarah, are you mad at us for teasing you on the bus?"

"Gosh, no. It was cute." Sarah sank deeper under the water.

Addressing Amina and Aashka, Sarah asked, "Are your parents in a rush to marry you like Dahabo's dad?"

Amina shrugged. "Not sure. They talk about education for one minute. Then, when a girl from our village gets married off, they say getting a man and having a family is important."

"Same." Aashka nodded her head. "After the last attack on our village, my dad sent my older sister off with a boy. He arranged with the boy's dad to keep her safe. She's married with two kids and another on the way. I never get to see her. My dad got money to help me stay in school. . . for now."

"My sister got thrown out of school for being pregnant. My parents lost the money they paid for fees." Amina shared. "She married and now spends her day collecting clean water and raising her children. I don't see her very often either."

Sarah's heart bled for these girls. "She was thrown out because she was pregnant?" Her voice was filled with disdain.

"I be a good wife. His dad say 'no' cuz I no speak English good." Dahabo's sad voice was too much for Sarah.

"I'm sorry." Sarah's useless sentiment was all she could conjure up at the moment. "What will happen if they find out?"

Dahabo and Amina's eyes widened, and the fear Sarah saw on their faces made her stomach writhe. "I be told to go with him," Dahabo claimed.

That would be a good thing, except her family wasn't the issue. Sarah felt helpless. She only had a few days left before heading back to the States. Besides, who was she to tell anyone how to raise their child? Just because Sarah disagreed with it, that didn't matter. This was their world, their way of living. All she knew was how much pain this situation was causing Dahabo, and that caused Sarah frustration and pain.

The hot spring was quieter than Sarah thought it would be. She spent the morning with the trio of girls who quickly became her favorites. Yes, teachers have favorites. They'll never admit it, but you can tell. After lunch,

Sarah found herself back in the same lagoon, holding onto the same rope so the current didn't wash her away. But this time, she was all alone. Her triad was swinging from the Tarzan rope. Well, Dahabo was cheering everyone on as she observed.

"Mind if I join you?"

Sarah's eyes bolted open at the sound of that deep, throaty voice. She knew that voice. It belonged to the man she hadn't seen all day, the one she made herself look ridiculous in front of. It was none other than her painfully handsome ex-fiancé, who clearly had zero interest in rekindling their love, regardless of what he said.

"Sure." Sarah's voice, barely above a whisper.

Under no circumstances was she to look in his eyes or at his bare chest, which she could see in her peripheral vision. Seeing his bare chest once a day was plenty. But her resolve was starting to crumble. At least in the tent, she could roll over and avoid him.

Sarah was keenly aware of the magnet pulling her toward Brandon. Sadly, she wondered if they were the same poles. It's impossible to connect matching magnetic poles. Within inches of contact, they repel against each other every time. For the last few days, Sarah had spent every waking moment hoping Brandon would drop his guard. Then, as she rested in the bits of the warmth of Brandon's arms, her daydreams came to life every night. Their nearness elicited too many feel-good sensations – Sarah was overwhelmed. If she could just feel Brandon's lips one more time. . . the sentence died in Sarah's head, knowing full well that one more kiss would never be enough.

"Mind if I grab on?" Brandon tilted his head toward the same rope Sarah gripped, hoping to fight the current.

"S-sure." *You're a teacher, Sarah. Pull a few more vocabulary words from that brain of yours.*

While the current was no joke, hence the ropes, Sarah's heart thumped wildly, threatening to bust through her chest. She understood why people who witnessed accidents could never get the facts straight. Adrenaline was a bullet train running through her body at alarming speeds, blocking her ability to think. *Breathe,* she coached.

"Are you okay?" As Brandon grabbed the rope, his bare chest — the extremely muscular one she wasn't supposed to pay attention to — brushed up against her shoulder.

Alright, Lord. There's a Bible verse that speaks about widows living their lives. She should have read this years ago and saved both of them the heartache. Sarah calmed her brain, trying to retrieve the verse she had once memorized:

I wish that all men were as I am. But each man has his own gift from God; one has this gift, another has that. Now, to the unmarried and the widows, I say: It is good for them to stay unmarried, as I am. But if they cannot control themselves, they should marry, for it is better to marry than to burn with passion.

Help me, Lord.

"I'm fine. How's your day been?" Sarah, proud of herself for forming a complete sentence, finally shifted her gaze from Brandon's display of years of hard work to his God-given, heart-stopping face. *Breathe.*

Brandon's knowing smile made Sarah blush. "I'm better now that I'm here with you," he said.

That sounded like flirting to Sarah. What had changed from the bus ride to now? Maybe, just maybe, Sarah wouldn't have to burn with passion any longer for the beautiful creation in front of her — only time would tell.

13

This might have been a bad idea, but Brandon didn't care anymore. The only regret he had was this miserable current. He should have chosen someplace else to reveal his feelings for Sarah, but his dad always said, *'When there's a will, there's a way.'*

It was true. Sarah had caught him off guard when she asked him to kiss her on the bus. Had shock not paralyzed his tongue, he would have responded with a resounding *yes!* He wondered where her brain was at. Did she think he'd rejected her...again? Hopefully, the time apart hadn't led Sarah to believe he didn't love her. He definitely did!

Sarah gently guided her hand up his bicep and shoulder, leaving a trail of pins and needles in her wake. He didn't flinch this time, but an inferno erupted inside him. Oh, how he'd longed for Sarah's touch. She massaged the tension from his neck like she always used to do. Her touch was divine.

"Have you been to a hot spring before?" Brandon blurted out, unsure where to start this conversation, trying to recapture cohesive thoughts.

Sarah shook her head. "This is a first." She drifted slightly to the right, but Brandon grabbed her free wrist.

"You can hold on to me too. I won't let you go anywhere." Based on Sarah's raised eyebrows, she was questioning the full meaning of that statement. "Yeah, I mean for that to extend beyond this lagoon."

Brandon gently pulled her closer. Sarah delicately pulled her hand from his embrace and clutched onto his bicep. Their eyes never parted from one another. The look in her eyes released a shot of adrenaline throughout his insides. "Sarah, I've never stopped loving you."

Wrapping his free arm around her waist, he hoisted her up. Their chests and thighs pressed tightly together. Now, at eye level, he couldn't help but notice the golden flecks scattered throughout her warm blue eyes, revealing pools of love and kindness.

Sarah may not have spoken a word, but her eyes told Brandon everything he needed to know. *She wanted him to kiss her as much as he wanted to.*

When they were only mere inches apart, Sarah whispered, "Brandon." Her soft, almost sensual tone jolted him to the core. Man, he loved the way his name sounded on her lips.

As Sarah opened her mouth to speak, Brandon captured her lips. He felt their heat bubbling between them as his lips swam over Sarah's with an urgency he'd harbored for the last five years. A soft sigh escaped Sarah, encouraging him to continue. Nudging her head to the side with his cheek, Brandon trailed kisses down the length of her neck and over her collarbone.

Like a bolt of lightning, a direction came from within — *stop, don't lose your honor!* Instantly, Brandon straightened up. "I'm sorry, I got carried away."

"Yeah, I know what you mean." Sarah's petite fingers pressed to her lips.

The simple motion had Brandon's mind swirling. Thoughts of securing those semi-swollen, pink lips again inflamed his insides with want and desire. Shaking those thoughts free, he rested his forehead on Sarah's. "I've missed you."

Without a word, Sarah let go of the rope and wound her arms over his defined shoulders, securing them behind his neck. She wrapped her legs around his torso, using him as a sturdy anchor, ensuring the current wouldn't wash her away.

Brandon let a low growl escape into her hair as he nuzzled his face into the side of her neck. *To heck with worrying about being rejected.* Who was he kidding? Brandon would risk being rejected again to have Sarah for a few brief moments. Of course, he wouldn't tell her that. *Thank you, Lord, for this woman.*

"Don't let go of me." Sarah's almost whimper encouraged him to grip her tighter. "I'm sorry I caused the separation between us. If you don't want to rebuild, I understand."

Brandon grinned. "I get it; you can't resist all this." She'd always liked his cocky teasing. Hopefully, she still did.

"You keep telling yourself that, Taylor." It'd been so long since Sarah had called him by his last name. He loved the way his name rolled off her tongue, but when his last name came out of her mouth, it gave him jolts of electricity to his heart.

"You didn't deny it." Brandon pressed on.

Sarah grabbed the rope and dropped her legs. Instantly, the hot spring felt like an ice bath. Enthusiasm filled her face as she wrapped her legs around the rope to steady herself. "You're right, I didn't," she said, throwing her hair up in a messy bun, challenging him with her eyes.

The water felt like lava again. Brandon returned her intent stare with one of his own as his entire body heated beyond a healthy temperature. *Did she say what I think she did?* During one of their nightly tent chats, Sarah had tried to assure him that her calling off the wedding had nothing to do with him. He hadn't believed her entirely, but the way she was looking at him right now, there wasn't a doubt in his mind that she cared for him. His gaze dropped to her lips and back up.

Loud children racing to the lagoon and jumping in from all sides captured the couple's attention. He knew the kid's presence should keep him from his next move, but it'd been too long, and his mind was set. Brandon pulled her soft body against his bare chest and slowly lowered his head. Brandon whispered within an inch of her lips, "Sarah, I love you."

"I love you too." Sarah snaked her arms back around his shoulders and played with the hair at the nape of his neck. Their lips barely grazed each other when Jimmy jumped into the lagoon, cannonball style, only a foot away from them. Sarah gasped. When Jimmy broke through the water, she splashed him until he begged for mercy. Brandon tugged on Sarah as the current caused her to drift away.

"It's time to get back to the bus and get these kids home." Jimmy's grin and knowing looks irritated Brandon. If he saw that Brandon was going to kiss his woman, why didn't he wait? That's alright. God willing, there will be plenty of time to pick up where they left off this evening.

Out of the corner of his eye, Brandon saw Dahabo grab Adolphe's arm as she almost fainted for the second time today. "Get her some water from that cooler!" Sarah yelled toward our crew as she swam toward the ladder, climbed it, and raced toward the young girl.

As Brandon joined Sarah, he inquired, "Who are you texting?"

"Lily. I want her to examine Dahabo."

Adolphe rested his knee on the ground, bringing him eye-level with the couple, "No, please. We don't want trouble."

"Lily is my daughter. You can trust her. I'm on your side, Adolphe."

Brandon scrunched his brows together. "What are you two talking about? Sides? Is there a fight?"

Adolphe and Sarah shared a look of concern that made Brandon's heart race. What did they know that he didn't? Sarah had always been the quick one. She never needed many clues to solve a riddle. Most of the time, she finished his sentences because she already knew what he was thinking. Clearly, she hadn't lost that ability.

Sarah's eyes asked Adolphe a question. He nodded. Turning to Brandon, Sarah rested her hand on his forearm. That sent a quick zap through his skin, but he tried to focus on Sarah's words. Which he knew he must have heard wrong.

Lily and Dahabo were in Lily's room at the host's house. Adolphe and Brandon were pacing outside the door while Sarah brought both of them a drink. "I think you two should sit before you wear the floor out."

"Thank you," They said in unison as they reached for the drinks.

The door creaked open, and Lily emerged. "Here's the deal. She's dehydrated. An IV would be the fastest way to get fluids into her, but we need parental consent, and she doesn't want me to contact them. Kurt is having her drink now."

Lily's no-nonsense, take-charge disposition filled Brandon with pride. She had transitioned from a feisty seventeen-year-old to an intelligent doctor who cared for her patients. As much as he hated the idea of her traveling the world with Doctors without Borders, he knew that the world needed her.

"The bigger problem is that she needs regular care. Am I to assume you are the father?"

Brandon turned white. He snapped his jaw shut while the rest of his body remained stone still. *He had heard Sarah correctly. Oh gosh, this isn't good!*

"Yes, I am." Adolphe's clear, crisp voice echoed in the small space.

Lily's eyes softened. "Can you explain why her parents don't know?"

"If they know, she will have to drop out of school. If my parents know there will be big trouble." Adolphe shook his head right before he gulped down his water.

Upon seeing Lily's brows crunch together, one corner of Brandon's mouth lifted, realizing he finally knew something was going on. However, his melancholy tone revealed the pain he felt for the kids. "Unless Dahabo can speak English, Adolphe's dad will not let him marry her. If this scandal comes out, the kids will be disowned from their families."

"How's she doing with her English, Mom?"

Sarah's lack of enthusiasm said it all. "Dahabo has made the most progress of any student thus far, but she still has more work before I think someone would consider her fluent."

Adolphe asked to see Dahabo. Without reservation, Lily took the young man into the room to see the mother of his child.

Meanwhile, Brandon sat beside Sarah on the bench so their thighs touched. He gently enveloped her hand. They bowed their heads to pray. "Lord, we pray for protection over the young couple and their unborn baby. You already know the outcome; Lord, we thank you for that. We ask right now for wisdom. Please provide us with your will so we can advise and guide this young couple. Please watch over the unborn baby. Keep him or her healthy, as well as Dahabo. Lord, please guide Lily, Kurt, and the rest of the medical staff's hands as they treat the young mom. In Jesus' name, Amen."

As the blue sky transformed into brilliant red and orange hues, Sarah's sober expression seemed plastered onyes her face. "If Amina, Aashka, and I worked solely with Dahabo and Rhys and focused on the other girls' English, I bet we could get her fluent(ish) before we leave."

Brandon squeezed her hand. "That's my girl. Always with a plan to help." He froze when he realized what he said. "I-I didn't mean *my*, and you're definitely not a *girl.*" He sputtered through without truly taking anything back from his statement. Why would he? He wanted Sarah to be his, so the statement fit as far as he was concerned.

Sarah ran her fingertips up and down his forearm before resting her head on his shoulder, lacing her fingers with his. "Can we put off the fun weekend? I feel led to help Dahabo and Adolphe."

Brandon would be lying if he said that his first answer was *No, we can't put it off*. He rebuked himself for his selfish thoughts. "Of course, as long as we get some time together before we leave."

"That sounds nice." With a tone of sympathy, Sarah lifted her head and asked, "What will happen to the three of them if Adolphe's dad doesn't accept her?"

"I'm not sure, love."

Just then, Adolphe emerged from the room. Brandon felt for the teen. That downtrodden, defeated look he saw on Adolphe's face was the same one that had been staring back at him in the mirror for the last five years. Brandon knew what it felt like to lose the love of his life. He didn't want to see that happen to the young man.

"I have to go home because my brothers are alone. Will you please make sure Dahabo gets home safely?"

Bewilderment filled Brandon and Sarah's faces. How did Adolphe expect them to get Dahabo home? They didn't know where she lived. Dahabo traveled to and fro with Amina and Aashka every morning and every afternoon. Too bad one of the girls hadn't stayed behind.

Brandon's heart felt like a ping-pong ball. It ached for the young man who was in a tough spot. He would do everything he could to help him. Yet, it was also filled with joy, knowing that Sarah still loved him.

"Of course. Get home to your brothers. We'll make sure Dahabo is safe." Sarah assured Adolphe with her words and a hug.

After checking on the young mom-to-be, Sarah and Brandon trekked to Amina's home. There, she convinced the teen to help Dahabo home. "Do all fathers have the same mindset as Adolphe's dad?" Sarah questioned.

Amina chuckled. "Yes, *my father made sure I could speak English because he didn't want me to get passed over like my sister did. 'When you know English, you have the world at your fingertips,' is what my dad always says.*" Amina rolled her eyes, seemingly not sharing her father's belief.

Brandon struggled to understand the reasoning behind the patriarchs' philosophy, but he didn't push the issue. People are always drawn to what they can't have, so why parents put added expectations on their kids baffled him. Brandon knew all too well what it was like to have a father piling the pressure on his back. His heart stung thinking of the arguments he and his dad had had over the years about Brandon not living up to his potential. He'd always thought his dad would be happy for him if he had a successful business. He did, but that wasn't enough for Caleb Taylor. Brandon wasn't opposed to hiring other contractors to work for him. Lord knows there are enough jobs that need to get done. Brandon's problem was finding the same quality of craftsmanship he expected from himself in other's work. He'd work alone until he found one or two more contractors who produced very high-caliber work. God carried him through every job he had for the past eighteen years, which worked for Brandon.

By the time they returned to Dahabo, she acted like a different person. Her energy level was up, and her once pale face now beamed with color. "Tank you for help." She smiled at Lily, who sent her home with an eight-pack of Gatorade.

"Remember, this is for you. It's okay to share, but you should have at least half of these before morning. Keep drinking clean water, too." Lily ordered, her voice filled with care and compassion. "Since we won't see you tomorrow, you must remind yourself to drink."

"I can help her remember," Amina assured the doctor.

As the girls strolled away, Brandon mulled over this afternoon's events. The great shock factor, he thought, was that Sarah still loved him. Dahabo, being five months pregnant, flabbergasted him beyond words. He and Sarah had a lot to talk about tonight, but hopefully, there'd be time for more kissing.

14

Heaven. This had to be what heaven felt like. Sarah's head and hand rested on Brandon's bare chest. His arm enveloped her like a cocoon, flushing her against his side. Silence filled the tent. Not the awkward silence between two people who didn't know or didn't like each other. No. A comfortable, protective silence shared only between people in love. *Brandon said he still loved me. I still love him too. Does that mean we're going to try being a couple again?*

Sarah looked up at the man she had planned to marry five years ago. His thick black hair hadn't thinned; it felt as smooth through her fingers as before. The day's worth of stubble increased his vigor, making him even more attractive to Sarah. What had she been thinking when she walked away? Clearly, she hadn't been!

"I'm sorry I was such a coward five years ago. I took as much from you as I did myself. I am not sure why I let my guilt and fears convince me that I shouldn't have been getting married." Sarah propped herself up on her elbow. She stared directly into his dark chocolate eyes.

He studied her. "What are you thinking, Sarah?"

"You're so wonderful. This time apart has been good to you in every way." Sarah's cheeks warmed as she shared her thoughts.

"What do you mean?" A slow grin spread across his face. He had to know what she was thinking, but he would make her spell it out.

"You're huge now, and I suppose it looks good on you if you're into having mounds of muscle..." Sarah waved her free hand up and down his core "...everywhere." Now, her face was on fire. *"This girl is on fire..."* Sarah only knew that one line from the song, but it fit.

"It only matters to me if you're into 'mounds of muscle everywhere,' are you?"

"On you, definitely."

Sarah didn't know how much more flirting her heart could handle before it burst from her chest. Brandon must have been thinking the same thing. He weaved his hands through her hair and gently tugged the back of her neck toward him. Their warm breath mingled together long enough for Brandon to whisper, "Oh, Sarah."

He pressed his lips to hers. The moment they met, Sarah relished in Brandon's full, demanding lips, deepening the kiss right away. Brandon let out a little growl when Sarah kissed his neck. Her soft kisses followed the vein leading to his jaw before her lips captured his again. Brandon pressed Sarah to the ground, and he returned her kiss with abandon. Even if Brandon hadn't told her earlier that he still loved her, she would have known from this kiss. The added weight from his upper body pinned Sarah to the down, warming her like a fleece-lined blanket. Sarah hoped this meant he forgave her, and they could move on.

Abruptly, Brandon pulled his lips away from Sarah's. He hung his head briefly before meeting her eyes, breathing heavily, and said, "I'm sorry, Sarah."

Sorry? Her body tingled from head to toe, and her heart sped like a meteoroid across the starry sky. *That wasn't anything to be sorry for.* Sarah placed her hands on either side of his face and hungrily captured his lips. For the next few moments, she savored the feel of this man's lips and weight pressing on her before she swiftly pushed his chest off her. "We need to stop before we don't. The last thing I need is more guilt to keep us apart."

Brandon laughed as he rolled onto his back. "No more guilt." Given the tight quarters, Sarah would have to snuggle up to the man she loved. As pleasant as that sounded, she needed a little space to get herself under control.

Excitement swirled through her chest. "How about we do something else to pass the time?" Sarah looked over at Brandon, who cocked an eyebrow at her. "Never have I ever." Sarah learned this from her students one year, and since then, she has played it during the first week of school to help the kids get to know each other.

"That sounds like fun. What does the person have to do if they have done it?" He paused for a few minutes. "The person who has done it will have to kiss the other person."

Sarah laughed. "How will that help with our current need for space to calm down?"

"I couldn't think of anything else." Brandon shrugged and grinned, his eyes beaming at her playfully.

Sarah's palm rested gently on his cheek. He leaned into her hand. "Okay," she agreed. "We'll do it your way." His full smile filled her with joy.

She giggled and wiggled her body sideways. Sarah faced Brandon, who was propped up on his irresistible forearm. *Since when was a man's forearm irresistible?* She was in too deep!

"Never have I ever done a hundred pushups in one workout session." Sarah thought she might have got Brandon on this one, but she wasn't sure.

"I have." Brandon waggled his eyebrows as he straightened his arm and leaned in for his kiss. Sarah wouldn't complain, but he definitely lingered longer than she'd expected.

Coming to a seated position, Brandon stared intently at Sarah as if trying to think of a particular question. "Never have I ever gotten a real tattoo."

"Come here for your kiss, big guy." Sarah leaned forward and put her hands on Brandon's strong shoulders.

"Whoa. Hold up. You have a tattoo? I seem to recall a certain young doctor who wanted to get a tattoo, and her mom told her that tattoos were not meant for a believer."

Dang him and his excellent memory. Weren't men supposed to forget everything? "Yes, I did say that." There was no point in denying it. Kids without God do stupid things. Heck, believers do stupid things sometimes. If she only knew then what she knew now. I bet there wasn't an adult alive who hadn't said that phrase.

"When we know better, we do better," was all Sarah could say. "Do you want your kiss or not?"

"Yeah, of course, but now I want to know more about that tattoo." Brandon stole another prolonged kiss.

"Never have I ever been on a yacht." Sarah tried to bulldoze right over the last round. She didn't want to revisit the poor decision she'd made during a game of truth or dare she'd played during her first year of college. That was her first and last time playing the game. Never again!

Brandon, lost in thought, still hadn't answered. Sarah waved her hand in front of his face. "Are you with me?"

Shaking his head, Brandon responded in a husky voice, "Sorry. I'm still thinking about that tattoo." Sarah swatted him on the arm. "What was the statement?" Sarah swatted him again, rolling her eyes and giggling.

"I have," Brandon replied after Sarah repeated her declaration.

Looking shocked, Sarah asked, "When did you go on a yacht?"

"Back in high school. Becki Landry's family was beyond wealthy. I don't remember what her dad owned, but he was the Jeff Bezos of the day. She invited me on a day trip with her family. We sailed from sun up to sun down." Brandon shrugged his shoulders like it wasn't a big deal.

"Were you two an item?" Why Sarah cared to know was beyond her, but she liked to know every detail about everything.

Brandon tipped his head. "I guess you could say that. We went out a couple of times, but nothing came of it. Obviously. She was too full of herself, so I didn't stick around long."

"It's your turn." Sarah rested her chin in her palms, waiting for the next round.

"I have to go to bed after this. I didn't get a kiss on that last one, so this one has to be good." Brandon pulled her onto his lap. "Come here." She let out a little squeal before settling. "You are my world, Sarah Morris." It pained her that her last name wasn't Taylor, but with any luck, it would be soon. "Thank you for agreeing to come here. Reuniting with you has been the second-best thing in my life."

"The second?"

Brandon tilted her chin up. His calloused hands felt gentle on her soft skin. Since he'd kissed her in the lagoon, that's all her mind could think of.

"Yeah, the first was when I met you all those years ago." Brandon's smile reached his ears, and Sarah's adrenaline kick-started her heart. The speed at which it ran through her system lit up her insides. His lips gently brushed hers at first, matching soft kiss for soft kiss. Then Brandon moved his hand to the back of her head and tilted it slightly to deepen the kiss.

And just like that, the kiss ended. "Sorry. Go back to your own side. We can't start that again." His sprightly tone made her snicker.

"Okay." Brandon worked to get serious, wiping his palms down the length of his face. "Never have I ever gone on an authentic safari."

"Me either."

"Tomorrow, you will. I've made plans for us to go to Saadani National Park. We have to get up early, and we won't be home until late, so those annoying gnats out there may get us."

Sarah wailed and wrapped her arms around Brandon's shoulders. "Thank you so much. I've always wanted to go on a safari."

"Me too. The best part is that we get to experience it together. We must get some sleep."

"Like that's going to happen. I'm too excited to sleep." Sarah huffed as she collapsed onto her back.

"Come here, Love." Brandon pulled her onto his chest, wrapping her in his arm. She leaned into his side and rested her hand near her face. Despite being the only way they could sleep in this cramped tent, Sarah would choose this every time. Brandon's muscular arms made her feel loved. As he dragged his fingers through her hair, warm sensations ran down her spine, causing her to shiver.

"Are you cold?" Brandon's voice, full of sincerity, made her smile.

"Definitely not." Sarah dragged her fingers over his chest.

Sarah couldn't believe the change she'd seen in Brandon over the past week. His haunted, hurt-filled eyes that she stared at on the plane were now kind, loving, and often alluring. It took Sarah's breath away to think about finding true love twice in her life. Instead of feeling guilty, which her dad always told her was a wasted emotion, Sarah needed to feel blessed that God loved her so much that He gave her another man to spend the rest of her days on earth with. She just might love this man more than she ever had.

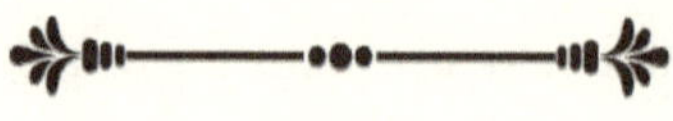

15

Brandon wasted no time getting him and Sarah into a four-by-four jeep, bouncing about and looking at the animals. Having Sarah seated next to him, their thighs banging into each other when the jeep tires met the ruts in the trail, was the best feeling in the world to Brandon. His backside would disagree, but what did it know?

"Oh, look!" Sarah leaned over into Brandon's space, pointing. "There's a warthog." They'd already seen a yellow baboon, elephants, and giraffes. The baby giraffes had been taller than Sarah, and Brandon was sure to tell her. It got him a playful swat on the arm, but he didn't care. Flirting with Sarah was definitely his favorite pastime.

With her cheek so close to his face, Brandon couldn't help himself. He leaned in and kissed her cheek.

"What was that for?" her voice soft and full of awe.

Brandon smiled and shrugged. "No reason." He'd remembered so many years ago when Sarah told him that a kiss on the cheek or forehead was 'super sweet and a way to get her attention.' He'd never forgotten that, and based on her reaction, her words still rang true today. "Hey, look, that's a lot of lions."

Sarah turned away from Brandon's side. "Oh man, that's a big pride. Look at those cubs. They're so cute."

Brandon leaned in again and whispered into her hair. "Not as cute as you." He bopped her on the nose with his index finger. *Where in the world did that come from?* Brandon was all out of sorts this morning. After almost pushing things too far last night in a tent made for Webster (he loved that old 80s sitcom), he had to sleep cuddling up to Sarah all night. That wouldn't have bothered him if they'd been married five years ago, but they hadn't, and quite frankly, Brandon was struggling. He gravitated toward Sarah like a moth to a flame. Keeping his honor intact and hers had grown increasingly more challenging the last few days.

Once their tour guide parked the jeep, the patrons exited. Brandon reached for Sarah's hand to help her up from her seat, but he never let go. His arm, slightly behind him, secured her hand as he led her to the front of the jeep. Once he bounded down the stairs, he turned and held his hand to Sarah like Prince Charming, asking for his lady's hand. He loved the flush in her neck and cheeks. Brandon wasn't about to let this woman disappear from his life again. He'd show her what she had been missing.

"Thank you, kind Sir." When she reached the ground, Sarah snuggled up close to him. He wrapped his arm around her shoulders, and she rested her arm around his waist. It felt perfect. "What's next?"

Brandon didn't care. He could walk like this — with her in his arms — for the rest of his life. Being in Africa was surreal, though; he wanted to ensure he experienced everything. "I thought we could change into our suits to prepare for our river tour. We leave in thirty minutes."

"Um, okay." Sarah's body stiffened slightly.

"What's wrong?" They crossed the path toward their locker, where they'd stored their bags when they arrived. "We don't have to do the river tour if you don't want to." Brandon didn't care that these tours were ridiculously expensive; he wouldn't do anything to make Sarah uncomfortable.

"I'll be fine. I'm just nervous." Sarah tugged on the corner of her lip. That caught Brandon's attention, turning his insides to liquid fire. Man, this woman was gorgeous. Her looks were only part of the reason he'd fallen for her. Her determination to succeed in everything she did was utterly attractive . . . on her. Some people take determination to an unhealthy level, but not Sarah — she used it to improve her life and the lives of those around her. Her determination would undoubtedly come in handy with the Dahabo and Adolphe situation.

He still couldn't believe what those poor kids were going through. This made him appreciate Lily, Kurt, and all the regular missionaries who regularly trek worldwide, instilling God into people's lives. There will never be a perfect answer because there is evil and temptation — oh, he knew the temptation — in the world, but things are better with God, at least; that had always been his experience. That's saying a lot since he was now faced with his ex-fiancé, with whom he was still head over heels in love and didn't have a clear picture of their future. But God knows; Brandon just needs to set time aside to ask.

"Anything I can protect you from?" Brandon's huskier-than-usual voice even surprised him.

Sarah turned to Brandon's side, resting her hand on his chest. He quietly sucked in a deep breath. The warmth from her hands seeped through his shirt's thin fabric, causing his chest to feel like he'd been branded. "Thank you. Your protectiveness is super sexy."

Brandon was surprised, and he couldn't suppress his smile. "I'll protect you from anything—even yourself—if you let me." He chuckled, hoping she wouldn't be upset by the last part.

Pushing up to her toes, Sarah gently kissed his cheek. "Crocodiles intrigue me, but the idea of being in the river with them doesn't make me real comfortable."

"Wait a minute. That's what you're nervous about?" Brandon held her shoulders away from his body so he could look at her. "Don't you live near the Everglades? What's it called Alligator Alley? Isn't there over a million alligators that live there?"

Sarah pushed out a laugh. "Actually, there's over a million alligators in Florida, but only a couple hundred thousand in the Everglades. Second of all," Sarah held up two fingers. "I don't go into the Everglades looking for them. I stay far away. Third," Sarah lifted another finger to indicate her final point, "we are not talking about alligators; these are crocodiles, and they are more vicious."

Brandon bit back a smile. "Mmm, hmm."

"Don't laugh at me." Sarah shoved his chest, but he didn't move. "Urg." Sarah turned toward the lockers, but Brandon wrapped her in his arms from behind. "I was just giving you a hard time. I'm sorry."

"It's okay. I'm not mad. I just don't have any defense against you. You're like a brick wall; I can't move you even a little bit. As long as you promise not to let me fall in the water, I'll go."

Now Brandon let out a boisterous laugh. "Did you think I'd toss you in? Of course, I'll keep you out of the water." Brandon squeezed her tight and hastily kissed her cheek. "I guess no snorkeling."

"Seriously? People do that in the river?" Sarah's jaw dropped. "I'm absolutely all set. I want to go home with all my limbs and my life today."

After changing, Sarah emerged from the changing quarters, tossing her bag back in her locker. Passing her bottle of lotion to Brandon, she asked, "Will you rub lotion on my back?"

"With pleasure." Brandon snatched the bottle playfully as he side-stepped behind her. Her beauty astonished him. The simple one-piece black swimsuit hugged every one of her curves. She'd let her blonde locks cascade down her shoulders, resting on her chest. The suit had crossed straps in the back, making her look sporty. His eyes roamed over the gaping hole at the small of her back. "You are gorgeous," he whispered close to her neck, shifting her hair to the opposite shoulder. The modest swimsuit left him still wondering where that tattoo could be. Brandon shook his head free of those thoughts and focused on lathering on the lotion. He hoped many more opportunities like this came along. In case they didn't, he would take his time massaging the coconut-smelling lotion into her soft, flawless skin.

When Sarah caught on to his lingering, she took the lotion back and thanked him for his help.

"Ready?" She asked after securing her locker.

"Absolutely!" Brandon reached for her hand. They headed to the beach. The tour guide told them they might be able to glimpse a female green turtle heading back into the ocean after laying her eggs. Sarah's soft, slender hands hid inside his large, calloused hands. He'd imagined the two of them walking hand in hand so many times. This moment felt so surreal. He never thought he'd walk anywhere with Sarah again, let alone in Africa. The fact that they had to fly to another continent to reunite was comical.

Unrest about his and Sarah's future filled his gut. Were they genuinely rekindling their love? Was their reuniting just because they were forced together? He'd meant to talk with her about it last night, but things had gotten carried away, and the conversation hadn't happened. Maybe he didn't want to know her intentions right now. *Would it be so wrong to enjoy this time and worry about the future when we complete our mission?*

"Oh, look, Brandon." Sarah pointed to the beachfront. "How many mother turtles are heading back into the ocean?"

"Too many to count. Wow." Brandon's voice was stunned by the sight of dozens of turtles.

Sarah pulled her phone out to take a picture. "Last year, I had a student who researched turtles. I helped him find a few videos. One of the things that stuck with me is the danger those little turtles face. It takes them about a month and a half to two months to hatch. They have to make their way from the shore to the ocean, avoiding predators like hawks. If they reach the water, fish and seabirds could still eat them."

Ducking her head, Sarah's cheeks were pink. "Sorry, I guess a lesson on sea turtles is unnecessary."

"Hey." Brandon tilted her chin toward him with his thumb and index finger. "I love hearing you talk about anything." He gently brushed his lips across hers. It'd been too long since they'd last kissed. He wasn't lying when he told her he liked to listen to her speak, but he loved kissing her, too. "I thought you were a dolphin fan?"

Sarah smiled. "Oh, I am, but after learning so much about turtles, I developed an appreciation for them as well. Dolphins are still my favorite, though." Now that the turtles were closer to the water, Sarah laced her fingers with Brandon's and strolled along. "I can't believe you remembered my love of dolphins."

A vivid memory of Sarah swimming with, feeding, and kissing a dolphin pierced his brain. "I've remembered everything." Brandon kissed the top of her head before he tenderly tugged her along, letting the sand sink under the weight of their feet.

Ugh, only ten people are waiting to ride this boat. They were sure to have a spot on the next vessel. Sarah crossed her arms as she and Brandon joined that line. Could she really ride this semi-rusty motorboat that looked like one swipe of a crocodile's tail, and it would capsize? She reminded herself that Brandon promised to protect her.

"What's the smile for?"

Shock filled her eyes. "I didn't know I was smiling." Sarah's arms released. Brandon must have taken the motion as an invitation. He stepped closer, invading her personal space.

His hands secured her arms. Gently guiding their bodies together, eliminating any previous gap, Brandon whispered in her ear, "Tell me, please," right before he dropped a lingering kiss on her cheek.

Sarah's shoulders shook when a chill filled her body. This man knew how to affect her. "I was thinking about you protecting me from the crocodiles when they turn this boat upside down." Sarah felt the rumble in his chest. She knew her paranoia was funny to him. Listening to him laugh, even if it was at her expense, set her heart ablaze.

He kissed the top of her head. "Don't worry. I will protect you," Brandon assured her.

The tour guide assured all the patron's safety as they boarded the boat. Yet here she was, praying as she'd never prayed before that God would watch over the entire boat and protect them from any wild animal attack. She imagined this man had conducted hundreds, if not thousands, of tours on this river, so if anything did happen, that would be God's will, right? *Lord, if your will is for a crocodile to kill me today, I can change your mind, right?*

Sarah had been so lost in her thoughts she jumped when Brandon wrapped his arm around her shoulders. "Would you calm down, please? We'll be fine." *Trust me.* The voice within was clear. I needed to trust God. He does everything for the good of those who love him. *Thank you, Lord. Please help me relax.*

She didn't know how much time had passed when she heard someone's excited voice from the back of the boat. "Hippos. Lots of them."

Brandon leaned into Sarah to see over the boat's edge. "If you would slide over, I could see the water too." A light laugh escaped him. His warm breath tickled her neck, and she shivered.

"Cold?" He knew she wasn't, but he liked to tease her. Just as Brandon pressed his thigh to hers, forcing her closer to the boat's wall, a cylinder emerged from the water about three feet from the boat. Brandon felt Sarah's body stiffen. He knew she'd seen what he had. The color drained from her face. The rise and fall of her chest increased. Brandon squeezed his arm around her shoulder and scooted her back toward his chest.

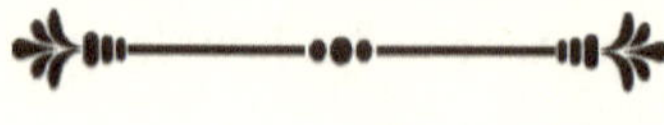

16

"Faith over fear," Sarah whispered to herself. If it was her time to meet her Creator, so be it. *Lord, I'm ready, but please don't let it be a crocodile that does me in.*

Her shoulders relaxed slightly when the figure disappeared underwater again. "How much longer?"

"We just started," Brandon let out a light laugh. "You do know it's rare for a crocodile to attack in the middle of the river, right?"

His response didn't answer her question, but she let it pass, knowing she probably didn't want to know how much time remained anyway. Sarah didn't answer Brandon's question either. Their guide told them crocodiles will attack animals, usually young ones, in the water. He watched a baby wildebeest get snatched up by a croc. It didn't help when he compared Sarah to the size of the young hoofed animal.

"The only thing I'm thinking about is that there are six hundred thousand crocodiles in Africa, and half of them are in Tanzania!" Sarah's inflection made Brandon chuckle again. That earned him a swat on the arm, which he laughed harder at when it obviously didn't hurt.

"It's the circle of life." Brandon shrugged.

"You don't mind that circle because you're the top dog," Sarah said, scooting her body closer.

The only good thing about seeing that crocodile was that Brandon now had her wrapped in his arms, shielding her from her scared state. She should probably thank that crocodile for revealing itself briefly. Brandon surely knew how to take her mind off things bothering her.

Happily, she sunk deeper into the space between his chest and bicep. He squeezed her tight, showing off his built-up biceps. They were impressive, revealing his commitment to being healthy. "So far, you've lived up to your word. I have all my limbs."

A light laugh escaped him. Brandon used his forefinger to lift her chin toward him. Their gazes locked — his soft, milk-chocolate circles held her attention. She saw adoration oozing from his eyes. He was all she needed. She pressed up, letting her lips slide across his softly. When she reached her arm up around his neck, he presumably forgot where he was and turned Sarah in toward him to deepen the kiss. No matter how many times he kissed her, she felt fire in her belly, swallowing up her ability to think straight.

Giggles in the distance suddenly jolted Sarah back to reality. She tenderly pushed his chest away. The shared look still lingered, but heavy breaths and goosebumps accompanied them. She added a chuckle when she saw the mother in the back of the boat covering her son's eyes. "A little more privacy would be better, don't ya think?" Sarah tucked a piece of hair behind her ear as she spun back, facing the water, still resting in his arms.

The tour guide called their attention to the monkeys feeding near the mangrove trees on the shoreline. "We have four species of monkeys here in the park. Black and white colobus monkeys, blue monkeys, vervet monkeys, and yellow baboons." He ticked off each one on his fingers. "The monkeys will rest in the trees or eat the small fruit, flowers, or shoots from the trees. The large canopy offers them protection from the crocodiles and African leopards."

Sarah side-eyed Brandon as if to say, *You've got to be kidding me, more deadly animals.*

Brandon kissed her temple tenderly, warming her thoroughly despite the cool breeze from the boat ride.

"Anyone want to touch a hippo?" the tour guide's excited voice burst from the speaker as he stood at the boat's helm.

"Yeah!" A set of twin boys, sitting at the bow with their mom, shouted.

The boat idled near a bloat of hippos. One of the twins reached over the metal rail on the side of the pontoon boat. His mother, understandably nervous, held a fistful of the boy's shirt. When the other twin reached over the side, she tried to grab his shirt, but he was too far away. She let out an anxious shrill, grabbing Brandon's attention. He bounded off the bench, reaching the boy just in time to plant his feet firmly on the boat floor.

"Go ahead, now. I've got you." Brandon smiled at the mother, who used both hands to secure her other son.

"Thank you, kind sir. It's hard when it's two against one."

Sarah giggled. She could only imagine the mother's pain. Sarah and Jake had only had one child. Lily was an angel of a child, comparatively speaking. She never had to worry about Lily falling overboard or getting hurt from outlandish shenanigans. God had been good to her in the child department.

"Alright, please take your seats. We're going to start moving again," the tour guide announced.

Brandon returned to the bench. His mahogany cologne greeted her as the breeze from the water gently blew her hair across her face.

"You are one of the good guys, aren't you, Brandon Taylor?"

A cocky grin plastered his face. He pulled his shirt from his chest. "You know it."

Sarah bumped her shoulder against him. "Get over yourself." Sarah let out a hard laugh.

"What? You don't think so now?"

Shrugging playfully, Sarah shook her head. "I just remembered you being more humble." Silence filled the space between them.

"Um...I...I'm sorry, I shouldn't have said anything." Sarah hated that she brought up the past. She'd been the one to walk away, creating this distance between them. She felt they'd moved on but hadn't made it official yet, so it was just an assumption.

A triumphant smile spread across Brandon's face. "Being humble didn't get me the woman I wanted, so I figured I should try cocky. Is it working?"

Leaning in, Sarah caught another whiff of his scent, sending her heart pitter-pattering to a new level. "I love every version of you." Her lips gently captured his. Evidently, his stiff lips hadn't expected the kiss.

Self-conscious, Sarah pulled back but didn't get far before Brandon clutched her shoulders. Guiding her back toward him, he seized her lips, immediately deepening the kiss. Her eyes fluttered shut. Their lips moved in rhythm. The spicy cinnamon taste from his gum teased her mouth. His gentle hands caressed her back, sending tingles down her spine. Her heart skipped a beat as he pulled her closer to his chest. The feel of his firm chest sent her heart skyrocketing even more. Sarah withdrew, sucking in a few deep breaths, trying to replenish her lungs.

"Wow," Sarah said in between breaths. She tucked a wisp of hair behind her ear, then quickly released it, looking around. Sarah felt heat rise in her neck. "The twin's mother is staring at us." Sarah flashed her an apologetic smile for making such a scene. To her surprise, the mother wagged her eyes, and her smile swallowed her face.

The boat approached the dock, indicating the end of the boat tour. "I hope you enjoyed this excursion. Feel free to visit the Mafui Sandbank, where you might see dolphins and humpback whales while you snorkel, admiring all the marine life of the Indian Ocean. If you've had enough of the water—"

Sarah pushed out a loud breath, louder than she expected. Her shoulders slumped. "Sorry."

The tour guide chuckled. "—The Zaraninge Forest has a closed canopy where you can see rare plants and animal life. Elephants have thrived in the forest for the last five months. They need the shade to survive the hot, humid, dry season."

A big bump, indicating the boat met the dock, lurched Sarah toward Brandon. "One kiss wasn't enough, huh?" Brandon grinned. "No need to throw yourself at me."

"Oh, brother. You're getting out of control." Sarah rolled her eyes.

Faux shock registered on his face. She studied the water, looking for wildlife, and ignored him. He grabbed her hand, regaining her attention. His warm hand enveloped hers as he guided her before him to exit the boat.

A foreign feeling filled her. Happiness. She hadn't felt this way since she'd pushed Brandon away. Now, it swirled in her stomach like a pinwheel.

While she waited for Brandon to talk with the twin boys and their mother, Sarah inspected the trees at the beginning of the dock. The leathery, dark green leaves were simple and soft. She'd never seen a tree's roots above ground except after a hurricane.

Her mind slipped back to Hurricane Charlie. They'd seen worse storms in Florida, but that one was memorable. Sarah was pregnant with Lily, due at any moment. She prayed that the hurricane would drift out to sea. She never asked for specific things because she knew God wasn't limited, so why restrict her options? Admittedly, she was scared something would go wrong with Lily's delivery if Sarah went into labor without a way to get to the hospital.

Fortunately, they'd made it through the worst of the storm, but the next day, Lily must have known something interesting was happening in the world. On the way to the hospital, Sarah focused on anything she could to keep her mind from the pain. Trees, hundreds of years old, in a horizontal position. Like the ones she stared at now, the roots were thick and intertwined.

Thinking of that day brought on a whole other set of emotions. Only a few hours after her first contraction, Sarah and Jake held their baby girl in her arms. He'd promised to protect and love Sarah and Lily until his dying day, right before he kissed her on the head.

A single tear fell, and she wiped it quickly, realizing that Jake had kept his promise. He loved, cared for, and protected Sarah and Lily until his dying day. The tree she was admiring turned fuzzy as tunnel vision took over. Simultaneously, Sarah's hearing became muffled. A bright light shone, blocking the tree from her vision. It reminded her of a multitude of rays illuminating from the sun, but brighter. The warmth from the light wrapped around her body. Instantly, an undeniable feeling came over her. It was as if God himself appeared to tell her to be thankful for Brandon. The last thing Sarah wanted was to seem ungrateful. She'd been blessed with a wonderful husband, who died at an early age, but now she knew that her life shouldn't have stopped when he died. She realized she was just as fortunate to have Brandon in her life.

Startled, Sarah jumped when Brandon's tone deepened next to her ear. He called her name and turned her toward him. Her sight and hearing returned to normal. "Where were you? It must have been an important thought. You didn't even feel me kiss you."

Her breath caught. "You just kissed me?" Sarah, voice questioning.

"Yeah, on the head. Who were you expecting?" Brandon let out a light chuckle before his lips turned down and his brows bunched together. "Are you okay?"

Brandon searched her face while she thought about how to respond. Was she okay? Yeah, she was better than okay, and it was time for him to know it.

They were close. An overwhelming urge to kiss him filled her entire being. He moved closer, tugging her to his chest. His strength was undeniable. Their breath mingled. *Kiss him.* A voice from within encouraged.

Sarah fisted the front of Brandon's shirt and pushed up to her toes. She wasted no time pressing her lips to his. She melted into him when her knees threatened to buckle. Her hands found his biceps and held on for dear life. He wrapped his arms around her waist, pulling her flush against his chest. She slid her hand up his neck to his jawline. The day-old stubble roughed up the softness of her palm.

The tree's shade kept their little make-out session semi-private. Brandon trailed kisses down her neck, leaving her skin tingling in his wake. He rested his forehead on her shoulder. Sarah's heavy breathing matched Brandon's chest's rapid rise and fall.

Releasing her for a moment, Brandon let out a light breath. "Wherever you just were, make sure you visit often." Then he winked at her and gave her a lingering kiss on the forehead.

She loved forehead kisses!

He remembered.

A chorus of women sighing *Aw!* danced through her head. Sarah tipped her head back and guffawed, "I've got permanent visitation rights, and I'm making you my honorary guest."

❖ ⦂⦂⦂ —————— •••• —————— ⦂⦂⦂ ❖

17

The next day, Brandon needed help to focus on teaching the boys to play soccer. He was in a state of euphoria. Everything reminded him of dandelions in bloom, allowing his time out with Sarah to invade his memory.

When they'd returned to their tent after their adventure, the gnats, thick as black clouds, filled the air. They quickly entered the tent. Wanting to change, Sarah had asked Brandon to face the opposite way. In the too-small tent, he was keenly aware of her every move. Brandon let out a low growl when she'd unzipped her jean shorts. *It might have been more safe if I stayed out with the gnats.* He squeezed his eyes shut and stuck his index fingers in his ears. He tried to think of anything except Sarah changing for bed. His mind strayed back to Sarah's tattoo — *definitely not a better thought. Please help me, Lord.* Brandon would respect Sarah until his dying day; however, he was a man after all, so he pressed his fingers even harder into his ears, hoping to block out every noise.

Brandon felt a gentle palm on his shoulder. He twisted his upper body and peeked out one eye. Sarah's angelic face stared back at him. Her knowing smile lit up his lower belly like a marshmallow pulled from the fire, with the orange glow of the fire turning the white flesh to charcoal.

Her hand slid down his arm, and they laced their fingers together. He pulled her to his chest, resting their connected hands together at the small of her back. "You are the most beautiful woman in the world." He leaned in slowly, stopping an inch from her lips. "Being with you is like a taste of heaven." Their lips met in a fiery passion at first. Then he slowed it down, relishing every inch of her full robe-bud lips. He got lost in the feel of her free hand massaging his scalp as Sarah ran her fingers through his hair.

As the seconds ticked by, Brandon slowly guided Sarah to the ground. Her arms wrapped around his neck, making the hair stand on its ends. He wrapped his arms around her waist and tugged her. She wouldn't get any closer unless she were on his lap. *Great idea, Taylor.* Brandon hoisted Sarah onto him. When she let out a muffled shriek, he smiled against her lips. She tastes like the fruit from the Babbob tree — sweet, citrusy, and spicy.

He deepened the kiss again before gently tugging on her bottom lip. Even the gnats' incessant buzzing faded in the distance despite knowing they were right outside the tent. At some point, he pulled the hair tie loose, and her hair cascaded down her shoulders. With a mind of their own, Brandon's fingers weaved through her thick blonde hair.

As much as Brandon wanted to savor this moment, they needed to discuss what these kisses meant. She lives in Florida; he lives in Maine. The idea of doing construction work in the Florida heat didn't appeal to him at all. Would he move so he could finally have a life with Sarah?

In a word, yes!

Could they slip right back to being engaged, or maybe they skipped right to the wedding? Every cell in his body hummed, liking that plan best. Though he tried to resist this coming together, it was futile. Being with Sarah was effortless and, quite frankly, the best part of life. There was no turning back now. He needed Sarah more than the air he breathed.

After another breathless make-out session, he spread his legs out and held his arm wide, creating space for Sarah to press her back up to his chest. Once she settled in, Brandon wrapped one arm around Sarah's shoulders.

He traced his fingertips up and down her bicep, caressing her silky skin with his other hand. Then, they spent the rest of the evening discussing what they wanted for their future. The memory of Sarah's face when he told her, *"You. I've always wanted you,"* threatened to melt his heart in a pool at his feet even now. He'd fallen quickly for her five years ago, and Brandon didn't need any reminders of how that ended for him. They hadn't been reunited that long, but he'd made it evident that he still loved her. By the way Sarah kissed him, she was still in love with him too.

Sarah seemed shell-shocked. Her eyes stared through him. Not knowing what she was thinking terrified him down to his marrow. People can enjoy a day out with someone but not want to spend the rest of their life with that person. Despite what Sarah had said about her leaving him before and how she kissed him with abandon, maybe he still needed to worry. Did second chances really work out, or was he headed for another heartache?

At that moment, Sarah had scooted closer, closing the gap between them; she threaded her arm through his and rested her head on his shoulder, his hand resting just above her knee. Wildberry raided his senses, and he kissed the top of her head. "I'm sorry for how I handled things, Brandon." she ran her fingertips up and down his forearm, sending little jolts of electricity through his veins. "You are my future. . ."

"Hey!" Jimmy yelling across the field brought Brandon back to the present. "Adolphe, take a break."

Brandon shrugged and held his hands to Jimmy, questioning what had happened. Both adults sprinted onto the field when Adolphe and Ring started to trade punches. Jimmy walked toward the other side of the field with Ring while Brandon took Adolphe the opposite way.

"Adolphe, take a walk with me," Brandon commanded the boy off the field.

Meanwhile, Sarah and Rhys ran toward them, all the girls at their heels. Brandon watched momentarily as Sarah spoke with the boys in the middle of the field. Hopefully, she would get to the bottom of what had happened.

Adolphe wasn't his usual self. Instead of dominating the field, the other boys were maneuvering the ball around him, and he wasn't running the field.

Stuffing his hands in the pockets of his athletic shorts, he studied the boy's face. "What's up? You are distracted and quiet today."

Adolphe mimicked Brandon's body language. "My dad introduced me to my future wife. I told him I love Dahabo. He refused to listen. He told me I must marry his wife in one week."

Shock smacked Brandon in the face. He rubbed his palm up and down the stubble on his cheek. "I don't even know what to say," he murmured.

"There is nothing you can say. There's nothing anyone can say. I have to tell my father she's pregnant." Adolphe shook his head.

Brandon queried, "What will happen when you tell him?"

Adolphe's silence made Brandon's stomach clench. He pressed his palm to the teen's shoulder, and they stopped suddenly. Then he asked, "Adolphe, what will happen if you tell your dad?"

"I'll never see her again." Adolphe's voice strained.

Brandon found that answer a little cryptic, but he accepted it at face value. "What would have to happen for your dad to accept her?"

"First, he said she had to speak English. Now he said nothing would make a difference." Brandon placed his hand on the teen's shoulder. The single tear that fell from the corner of Adolphe's eye touched Brandon.

"What can we do to help?" Brandon said, running his hand through his hair.

"They're doing it." Adolphe pointed to Sarah, Aashka, and Amina, who returned to working with Dahabo to perfect her English. "Will it be enough?"

"I don't know, Bud. But if Dahabo can speak better English, Sarah will make it happen." From across the field, Brandon and Sarah's eyes met. He couldn't read her expression. Were things going well, or were Adolphe and Dahabo destined for a life of misery?

Adolphe shook his head. "I need to play ball; forget this for now," he said, his eyes filled with tears.

"You need to apologize to Ring. I don't claim to know what happened, but given your stress, he didn't have to do much to get your punches swinging." As the teen took off toward the field to join Jimmy and the other boys, Brandon headed toward Sarah to check on the girl's progress.

Brandon felt helpless. After learning about Adolphe's situation, Brandon imagined himself going to the family's home and letting the teen's dad know the pain he had unnecessarily inflicted on his son. Only the boy's father could explain his rationale, but Brandon knew the father didn't owe him an explanation, and if he tried to help Adolphe, he might make things worse.

When he reached the crowd of girls, Brandon witnessed Adolphe and Ring shaking hands on the field. The way Adolphe was hanging his head and shaking it, Brandon knew the young man was accepting responsibility for his poor decision to fight with Ring.

"Hey." Sarah's face lit up with just one word. His insides melted. Brandon looked her over from her toned shoulders down to her pink-painted toes. "How's everything going?"

Her eyes drooped. "Slowly." Sarah pushed off the ground, and Brandon clutched onto her wrist, guiding her to her feet. They stepped away from the trio of girls. "I'm worried that no matter what we do, it won't be enough." Sarah shook her head. "Brandon, she's made so much progress already. What does Adolphe's dad want—for her to speak better English than you and me?"

"I won't pretend to understand." Brandon traced his knuckles down her cheek and tucked a loose tendril behind her ear. The only thing he knew at that moment was how badly he wanted to kiss Sarah and move on with their lives together as a couple. He felt terrible for his selfish thoughts. There would be time to convince Sarah Morris that she needed to be Sarah Taylor. Right now, he needed to focus on helping the teen couple. "How can I help?"

"We're doing everything we can already," Sarah said, her voice downtrodden. Brandon couldn't remember a time when Sarah sounded defeated. She'd always been willing to think of a new idea and try something new, but she seemed at a loss right now, which made Brandon nervous.

Sarah touched her palm to Brandon's cheek. Brandon leaned into it. "I better get back to them." Their gazes were locked. Heat and tingles filled his chest. She pushed up onto her toes and kissed his cheek.

"If you need me, just text." Brandon stepped back, and her hand dropped to her side. After a few strides back to his side of the field, he turned to see Sarah still staring at him. There was something different about Sarah this morning besides her slightly crushed spirit. Thankfully, he didn't have anything to do with that. Brandon would never understand the idea of a parent keeping two kids apart when they seem to be better together.

When he turned around, a sparkle in her eyes shone bright like the night stars. All he had ever dreamed about was Sarah returning to him, and now it seemed like he'd finally woken from a five-year-long nightmare without the woman who had completed him. A thought came to Brandon: how would he know if she was ready for the next step? He definitely didn't want to rush her again.

His willpower dwindled more and more as the day progressed. Brandon mentally chastised himself. Dahabo's learning English should have been his focus, but everything had changed since spending the day with Sarah. Protecting her from any potential crocodile mishap had his heart dancing. He hadn't worried about an actual problem with wildlife, but the opportunity to be close to Sarah had been worth the price of admission. Then the kissing, *wow*! Brandon had let himself fall entirely under Sarah's power. . . again. He needed to get Sarah to marry him, and he would if it was the last he did.

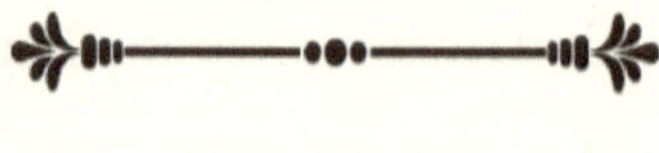

18

"Lily, what do you mean you can't treat her without parental consent?" Sarah asked, her voice raised, disrupting the peaceful tilt of the universe.

As they'd neared the end of the week, Sarah had noticed Dahabo growing weak. She'd complained of headaches and stomach sickness, which Sarah didn't think much about — those things are par for the course when one is pregnant.

Lily raised her hand to quiet Sarah. Fortunately, Sarah didn't take offense since this was Lily's territory. Lily was a confident, skilled doctor who deserved respect, and Sarah was and always will be a mom. Though Dahabo may not be her flesh and blood, she cared for this girl's well-being.

Lily lowered her hand and explained. "We aren't talking about life or death where we have authority to take action without consent. Dahabo needs an IV to get the nutrients she missed before we got her on prenatal vitamins."

Looking at Dahabo, Sarah inquired, "What will happen if you tell your mother about the situation?"

"She makes the boy marry me." The girl looked captivatingly at Adolphe. Based on his return look, Sarah felt like she was intruding on a private moment.

Sarah enjoyed listening to Dahabo's daily improvement in her English. She had come so far in the short time Sarah had known her.

"Lily, is there, um... any way around this?"

"Afraid not." Turning to Adolphe, Lily queried, "Have you tried sharing Dahabo's improved English with your dad?"

Adolphe hung his head. "He doesn't listen to me. He expects me to marry the wife he picked out."

Sarah shook her head. "When?"

"A week." Adolphe got choked up.

Apparently, Sarah needed to do more to help this couple, but what? If anyone thought they could stop Sarah from doing what she was currently thinking, they obviously didn't know her desire to help others, especially kids and young adults. "I'm going to talk to your father."

"No!" Adolphe roared. "Women don't tell men what to do here. Please, don't." He put his hands up, palms facing Sarah. "Brandon will kill me if anything happens to you."

Sarah appreciated Adolphe's warning and concern. A slight grin escaped her pursed lips, thinking about the teen's respect for Brandon. She hadn't thought of the cultural implications as her mind ran wild with the speech she would tell the patriarch. "Maybe Brandon will go talk with him, and in the meantime, we'll keep teaching Dahabo how to improve her English."

Turning to Lily, "How do we help Dahabo get what she needs from here on out?" Sarah contemplated.

"She should stay here overnight for observation, but without parental consent, I have to send her on her way," Lily said, her voice frustrated.

"I'm good. Aashka and Amina can walk home with me." Dahabo stated matter of factly.

After the teens left the clinic, Sarah let out a dramatic breath as she collapsed in a chair. "What are we going to do? Adolphe has to marry the woman his dad chose in a week. Dahabo needs medical treatment now. We can't let this go on any longer."

"Is there anything *we* can honestly do?" Brandon sympathized.

Sarah's heart dropped faster than the first descent on a roller coaster. She knew that Brandon was probably right — the teens would be the only ones who could change Adolphe's dad's mind.

"Why don't Adolphe and Dahabo just tell their parents that she is expecting? Won't that help him change his mind?"

Brandon shook his head and shrugged. "Adolphe doesn't seem to think so."

"We're leaving in a week. We need to find a way to unite the families so Adolphe's family can see Dahabo's progress and what a great provider Adolphe would be because he loves her." Sarah dropped her head into her hands. The feel of Brandon's warm palms rubbing her shoulders was heavenly.

Part of her wanted to ensure the teen couple were securely together before she left, knowing that life, thoughts, and feelings can get in the way of God's greatest plan. That was her guilt talking. God had set this handsome man in front of her five years ago, and she messed it all up by walking. It's clear to her that God was giving her a second chance. One of the most extraordinary things about God is that He never quits. Though Sarah missed up years ago, God put Brandon back in her life. This was their opportunity to finally be happy, and Sarah wanted the same for Adolphe and Dahabo.

"Mom, you can't save them all. Isn't that what you tell me?" Lily mocked her mother, using the exact words Sarah had used when Lily lost her first patient.

"True, but I haven't exhausted all resources yet," Sarah said confidently. Looking up at Brandon, she added, "We should get going."

"Thanks, Lily. We'll run it by you as soon as we develop a plan. Dahabo getting the medical attention she needs really should be our first concern." Brandon placed his palm on Sarah's back, warming her skin through her thin shirt.

"Good night, honey." Sarah hugged her daughter just as Kurt arrived home from his assignment. Watching him sneak up behind Lily and tickle her, making her giggle, made her heart smile. Knowing that her daughter was well loved, protected, and taken care of alleviated some stress. Mothers always worry about their kids, but she worried less with a son-in-law like Kurt.

Sarah settled into the tent while she waited for Brandon. He'd left his bag open, its contents spilling out. Her eyes caught on an envelope with her name on it. Against her better judgment, she opened the mail, noticing the date — five years ago this January. Brandon's relatively neat handwriting caused her stomach to hollow out. She braced herself for what might be a hate letter.

Dear Sarah,   *January 20, 2018*

I don't even know where to begin. You stole my heart like a thief in the night. I've already been through the cry-your-eyes-out stage and am now angry. I don't understand why. You disappeared, unwilling to explain why you left me. You're a coward. That is the last thing I ever thought you'd be in our time together.

If you don't love me anymore, I'll have to deal with that, but I don't imagine that is your reason for walking away. When people say that love conquers all, I believe that. You should have respected me enough to tell me what you thought and felt. We could have worked through it, but instead, you selfishly planned my future too.

I'm not waiting around for you. I would appreciate it if you could find it in your cold heart to tell me what prompted this separation.

Tears spilled down her cheeks as she reread the unfinished letter. She deserved all of that anger and more. Thinking about how the last five years had affected Brandon pierced her heart like a hot fire poker. Without Brandon, she had been miserable, too. Hopefully, she could heal some of the anger in Brandon's heart.

The tent flap whipped back, and Brandon entered. After securing the zipper, he locked eyes with Sarah. She knew her eyes had to be puffy and red. Sarah watched Brandon's gaze move back and forth between the contents of his open bag and the letter in her hand. A silent tension filled the small space.

"Sarah, I wrote that when I was angry. I'm sor—" his voice soft.

Disbelief washed over her. Not only had she caused the anger in this letter, but she had read the letter without his permission, and he was apologizing to her. Yeah, she definitely made a mistake not marrying him five years ago. "You have nothing to be sorry for; I do. Please forgive me. I saw my name on the envelope, and you know how I am with surprises." She smirked and shrugged slightly.

"Oh, I know. You don't do surprises." Brandon reached for the letter, crumpling it with one hand, and tossed it over his shoulder. He lay in his spot with open arms, welcoming her in.

Brandon wrapped his arm around her shoulders, pulling her close to his side. She rested her hand on his bare chest and drew circles with her fingertips. "You were right. I was a coward. I couldn't tell you that I felt guilty; I felt like I was betraying Jake's memory by moving on. I know I should have told you. Then I got it in my head that you'd be upset and leave anyway, so I left. I couldn't take the pain of losing another man I loved."

"You lost me because you left me. I know you loved Jake. You'll love Jake until you go home to be with Jesus. I'm never going to take that from you. I just wanted you to make room for me in your heart." He thought they'd already squashed this earlier, but being direct was the only way. "Is there enough space for me?"

Her tears created a small pool on Brandon's chest. "Sorry." She wiped it off with the sleeve of her sweatshirt.

"It's okay, Sweetheart. I'll take your tears on me anytime."

Sarah's pulse accelerated as she sat up. "My mind is all over the place." Her breath hitched when Brandon wrapped his arm around her shoulder and rested his other hand on her thigh.

Brandon lifted his knuckle under her chin until their eyes met. "I want to be with you forever. Florida is not my thing, but I'll move there if that means I finally get to marry you. Sarah, I've been miserable without you, but after spending this time with you, I don't want to return to being apart."

More tears fell. Brandon wiped them with his knuckle. "I already asked my dad if I could move back. I plan to go to Florida to sell my house and move back to my dad's."

Without hesitation, Brandon pulled Sarah into his arms. His calloused hands reminded her of how hard this man, *her* man, worked back home. "That's the best news I've heard...in the last five years." Light laughs escaped from both of them.

"Brandon," Sarah whispered, pulling away from his chest. "There's always room in my heart for you."

He reached into his bag and pulled out a familiar-looking box.

Sarah felt her heart rapped against her core. She couldn't think of a single reason to say anything other than yes, provided she was correct about the question he was about to ask. *Thank you, Lord, for this second chance.* The hand covering Sarah's mouth shook.

Time ticked by so slowly as Brandon opened the case. Then he pulled it out and inspected the stone. He squeezed his eyes shut; Sarah figured he was praying. She couldn't take it anymore. "Are you trying to torture me?" Butterflies vibrated throughout her stomach

His lips curved up, but then his eyes turned serious. "I'd never torture you." Brandon knelt on both knees. He took her face in his hands before he took her left hand and kissed her knuckles. "Sarah," his words came out in a hungry growl. "You are the love of my life. I've been one step above depression without you. I believe God is giving us a second chance. Will you marry me and allow me to show you how much I love you?"

His affectionate smile, alluring and lovely, increased her body temperature. She couldn't believe this. He still had the ring he'd offered her five years ago. She hurried to close the gap. Placing her palm on his cheek, he leaned in. "It will be an honor to marry you." Sarah tilted her chin up as Brandon leaned down. She pressed a gentle kiss to his lips.

Brandon pulled her back just enough to slip the ring on her finger. "It's my honor. I'll treat you like the gold on heaven's streets." She rested back on her heels, dizzy from the passionate way his eyes and words spoke to her.

He scooted back and let his fingertips trail down her arms. Goosebumps shadowed over her forearms, and he rubbed them briskly to dissolve them. "Should we get married tomorrow?" Brandon winked to show he was teasing. . .sort of.

"My dad would be so disappointed if he missed it, but we could perfect our kiss for the big day." Sarah gently tugged Brandon's biceps toward her.

Their lips danced together, matching kiss for kiss. This one was different from all the others.

"Please tell me we don't have to wait long. We've waited long enough to be together."

She may not be able to marry this man tomorrow, but she knew one thing: she wouldn't wait long before making this man her own. "We will be on the express train down the aisle."

"Now that's the best news I've heard," Brandon repeated the phrase, making Sarah giggle.

Her expression turned serious. "We can't leave Dahabo and Adolphe to get through this alone, even though we're supposed to head home in a week," Sarah said, wrapping her free arm around Brandon's waist and hugging him.

"What if we invite the families to dinner and share the news then?" Brandon suggested. "I mean, realistically, how much improvement can Dahabo make with her English in a week?"

"A lot if we keep helping her. She has the necessary motivation, so she doesn't truly need us; we just help her progress more quickly," Sarah said.

"Brandon, what's going to happen with us in a week?" Her voice, stilted and unsure.

19

Only two more days before this mission trip in Africa would be a distant memory. Tonight, they were having dinner in a separate, smaller room in Mustaf's home with Dahabo's and Adolphe's families. Lily had shared the situation with the area coordinator, Fardowsa, who explained the problem to the volunteer.

Brandon only had one interaction with Mustaf besides eating dinner at the host's home, but he could tell that the man had a heart for Jesus. He cared about the well-being of others, and that's what being a Christian is all about – sharing and loving others like Jesus did. He cared about the volunteers he housed during their time in the country just as much as he cared about the natives.

Apparently, Fardowsa had had run-ins with Adolphe's dad in the past, and Mustaf, the host who'd volunteered for a couple of decades, knew Adolphe's family well. Through that connection, the situation smoothed itself out. Brandon hoped they would be just as lucky this time around.

Today was their last day working with the kids. Tomorrow, they'd spend their time packing and preparing for the excruciatingly long plane ride home. Lily had thought of everything. She'd booked their return flights, anticipating that he and Sarah would be reconciled. Lily squealed with delight when they showed her the ring on Sarah's finger.

It will be an honor to marry you. Brandon struggled to focus on anything other than the words she'd spoken from her sweet-as-honey lips with love in her eyes.

Pride filled Brandon's chest as he caught a glimpse of his fiancée doing everything she could to help Dahabo speak English fluently. This was the last-ditch effort before the families gathered tonight. Brandon wasn't a linguist, but he'd noticed a vast improvement in the girl's speaking ability since they'd arrived; God willing, it was enough.

He didn't know what would count as enough in this culture. These kids dealt with more in a little over a decade of their lives than he had in a few decades. Today, the boys were playing manhunt, and what Brandon and his buddies referred to as a fun game was a survival game for these kids. Sadness permeated Brandon's soul when one of the younger boys, Omari, said, "We play this all the time when the bad guys come around." Evidently, his village had just been raided by rebels looking to expand their army. He'd watched his friend's older brother be beaten with the butt of a rifle and dragged away while his mama cried.

Brandon knew his life would never be the same. Playing manhunt at home in a safe, fun environment would make him think of Omari and the other kids hiding to stay alive. He knew people didn't always know why things happen or what their impact was on others, but Brandon hoped he'd made a difference in these kids' lives in the short time he was blessed to interact with them.

"How do you think tonight will go?" Jimmy queried as he and Brandon tried to camouflage in the bushes.

"I'm not sure. If Adolphe's family has to deal with anything like Omari's, I can kind of understand why they live and make the decisions they do."

Jimmy let out a long breath. "No kidding. We didn't even know it happened. How Omari came here the following day without acting differently is beyond me."

"Where are you and Rhys headed after this?" Brandon peeked around the bushes to see if they were any closer to being captured. No kids were in sight.

"We're heading home to finish the work for our Master's degrees and enjoy the time together before we return to school next fall. We've got a lot to plan for."

The broad smile on the man's face was barely contained. "Lily, just let Rhys know that she's pregnant."

The two men clasped hands and bumped their opposite shoulders. "Congratulations. I am so excited for you two. Will that mean the end of your mission trips?"

"Oh no, Rhys already said we'll do our first mission when the baby turns one. We'll see if she still feels that way when the time comes. My mom doesn't think she will, but Rhys is the most determined woman I've ever met."

"That must be why she and Sarah get along so well. I hope all their hard work pays off; Fardowsa doesn't seem to think it will." Brandon pressed his lips tight together and shook his head.

"If either of the families object to Dahabo and Adolphe marrying, then maybe they should just run away so they can be together."

Brandon chuckled softly. "This isn't a real-life Romeo and Juliet. If their families won't concede, they'll have to live with the consequences of telling them in just a few hours."

Distracted by their conversation, Brandon didn't hear the stealthy footsteps sneaking up on him until it was too late.

"Gotcha!" Omri yelled as he pulled the branch on the bush back to reveal their hiding place.

Jimmy headed toward the middle of the field, where all the other captives waited for the last kid to be found.

"I'm going to talk to Sarah." Brandon headed in the opposite direction. "Hey, Beautiful, how's it going?" Brandon inquired when he reached the group of girls with Sarah.

"Seeing how Adolphe's dad reacts to the news will be interesting. This might turn into the parent fighting and the kids being stuck in the middle."

Sarah shook her head. "Sadly, I think you're right."

Four hours later, Sarah, Brandon, Dahabo, Adolphe, and both sets of parents lined the perimeter of the host's rectangular table. They had practiced that Dahabo would engage in the conversation so her English would be known. Then, Adolphe would propose to Dahabo to start the discussion, but he was stalling.

Everything was going awry. Adolphe's dad must have sensed this because he mentioned Khadija, the woman he'd set Adolphe up to marry in a week. The stare-down that ensued between father and son filled the room with tension.

Brandon noticed that Sarah only moved the food around on her plate, making it look like she'd eaten something, but he knew better than that. Her anxiety-filled body wouldn't be able to eat. He placed his hand on her restless thigh that felt like a jackhammer on high. He leaned close to her ear and whispered, "Settle down, Sweetheart. I think things are going to get real right now." Brandon took another bite of his grilled fish slathered in coconut sauce. He nodded at the young man, encouraging him to begin the discussion.

Adolphe spoke, but not to his father. "This is the best fish I've ever tasted. Thank you, Mustaf."

"You're welcome." Turning to Adolphe, Mustaf asked, "Would you like me to give the recipe to Dahabo so she can cook this for you again?"

Way to go, Mustaf! Brandon smiled at the host, who nodded in return as if to say, "Glad I could help."

Multiple hands froze in the air, midway between plates and mouths. "Dahabo? Adolphe is marrying Khadija. What is the meaning of all this?" Adolphe's dad asked, waving his hand at the dinner spread, his tone irritated and impatient.

Adolphe didn't speak for a split second. Then, he stood and walked to the other side of the table, placing his hand on Dahabo's shoulder. "Dad, mom. I want to marry Dahabo."

"We've discussed this already, Son—"

"—Dad, you've heard her talking. She speaks better English than Mama. Besides, we haven't *discussed* anything. You've told me how *you* want things to go, but that's not what I want for my life."

"Maybe so, but Khadija's family already gave money. We are not giving it back."

Brandon's heart ached for the young man. His future held so much uncertainty. Instead of having his family's support, he had to fight them. He didn't expect the boy to be strong enough to finish the plan, but he surprised Brandon.

A gnawing feeling in Brandon's gut disturbed him. Adolphe's dad, on the surface, appeared to be hard-headed, but something seemed off to

Brandon. The man's eyes looked conflicted, almost pained to tell his son that he couldn't have what he wanted.

One look at Sarah, who was studying the older man as well, let him know that he must be on to something. Sarah could read people well.

"Dahabo and I are getting married tomorrow, and we will raise our baby together. If you want to be part of that, great; if not, that's your choice."

Time stood still. Everyone's eyes were like ping-pong balls, bouncing back and forth from Adolphe to his dad. Despite the silence in the room, Brandon watched Adolphe relax. His parents sat with their jaws hinged open. Surprisingly, Sarah sat with a slight smirk on her face. *What did she know that I didn't? She had to have a plan brewing in that pretty mind of hers.* When she dropped her hand on top of his, still resting on her thigh, she squeezed it, and he instantly knew – she was hopeful.

"She is the woman I want as my wife. I've already taken steps to show that she is mine and will be forever." Adolphe elaborated.

Realization finally hit Dahabo's parents — "She's pregnant?" Her mother squealed, which sounded like a happy excitement, but Brandon could be wrong.

Sarah's head shot back toward Adolphe's dad at the same time mine did. She hadn't said anything up to that point, but Brandon could tell she felt terrible how the news blindsided Adolphe's family and wouldn't stay quiet much longer.

"Are you okay, Sir?" Sarah asked, concerned. Adolphe's dad stood rapidly, knocking the chair to the floor.

He turned back to Sarah. "Would you be okay if you were me?" He asked with a distaste that had Brandon on his feet.

"Don't you dare speak to my woman that way!" Brandon's muscles tensed. He clenched his fists. It was bad enough this man was trying to ruin his own son's life, but he wouldn't speak to Sarah with anything but respect – he'd make sure of it.

Sarah was on her feet and whispered in his ear, "Don't let him get to you. You are better than that."

Steadying her gaze on Adolphe's dad, Sarah spoke her piece. "If you don't mind me saying, Dahabo will be a resourceful wife. She's learned to speak relatively fluent English in just a matter of weeks. That shows her intelligence and determination to marry your son."

Brandon felt proud. Sarah had always been the one to stand up for her students. She'd lost sleep over this situation, not that she would admit it to anyone, but he'd witnessed her distress firsthand.

Finally, the patriarch spoke. "Sarah, is it?" She nodded. He spoke low and articulated each word perfectly. "I cannot afford Adolphe's silly dream of marrying this girl."

"Your son got my daughter pregnant, and he's trying to do the right thing. Clearly, he learned morals from another family in the village." Dahabo's mother retorted. Brandon felt the metaphorical punch to the gut as if it had been addressed to him instead of Adolphe's dad.

"Mama!" Dahabo scolded her mother. Standing beside Adolphe, she thanked Mustaf for dinner and spoke directly to Adolphe's mom. Then she scanned the room, looking at her mom and finally landing her stare on Adolphe's dad. "If you can't accept that we love each other, you'll miss seeing your grandchildren."

She tugged on Adolphe's arm, guiding him to the door.

"Hassan! Do something." Adolphe's mother ordered.

"I will leave first." Hassan turned as he reached the door. "If you want to sign your father's death papers. Go ahead, marry this girl. I will not stay around for it."

Brandon felt awkward. He had expected the fathers to lead this meeting, but Dahabo and the mothers had taken over until now. As Hassan walked out the door, he ended the conversation, leaving everyone in shock and despair.

Sarah and Dahabo stared at one another; Brandon couldn't tell what they were saying, but they were definitely communicating. Then, Sarah excused herself, chasing after Hassan.

Dahabo's dad stood, shaking Brandon's hand, he thanked him for helping the teens as much as he could. "Hassan is a tough man. No one ever get through to him."

Adolphe's mom rested her head in her hands. Brandon rested his palm on her shoulder. Hopefully, that was a universal sign showing support. When Adolphe and Dahabo both comforted the woman, she started to cry.

"He's in big trouble. Owes big money to people. We get loan for other son."

"You take money for Abdul's medicine?" Adolphe seemed shocked. Brandon had thought Adolphe knew everything that happened in his household.

Tears poured down the older woman's face. Brandon's heart ached for this entire family, but worry gnawed at his gut. Where was Sarah? Would she be okay? Hassan wouldn't hurt her.

Ten more minutes passed. "I'm going to find Sarah," Brandon announced, unable to wait any longer. At the same time he reached the doorway to go out, Sarah entered with Hassan closing following behind her. She nodded her head toward the table where the families remained, and Sarah sidled up to Brandon.

He didn't know what was about to happen, but based on the peace shining on Sarah's face, he knew that, once again, she'd come through for her students. Though these two teens were more than students to both of them — they were friends.

Adolphe's dad stood at the edge of the table, staring at his and Dahabo's families. The silence was killing Brandon. He wanted to know what had happened between Hassan and Sarah. He leaned into her hair, "Is this going to be good or bad?"

"Ye of little faith." Sarah didn't answer him directly, but from what she *did* say, he knew the outcome would be good.

Hassan moved swiftly toward the couple. "Son, I will give the money back to Khadija's family. We don't want to lose you and our grandchild."

Cheers erupted! Hoots and hollers. Hugs, tears, and kisses filled the room. Dahabo and Adolphe approached Brandon and Sarah. "Thank you for all you did for us. I don't know how you got him to change his mind — he's stubborn — but thank you." Adolphe wrapped his arms tightly around Sarah.

"You've got your own woman to hug; let go of mine," Brandon joked with the teen, sticking out his hand for a firm handshake.

Three hours later, Brandon and Sarah finished cleaning up the mess from dinner with Mustaf and his wife. "Thank you for providing your home for this meal. It was so nice to see everything work out for them." Brandon shook the host's hand as Sarah strolled toward the door.

"It's nice to see things working out for you too." Mustaf tilted his chin toward the door where Sarah waited. "You, two, are good together. I hope to see you back here sometime."

"It would be our honor. Thank you," Brandon revered.

Brandon's heart raced as he met Sarah's gaze. His stomach filled with excitement and nerves. He'd been here before — engaged to the most beautiful woman in the world — and the fear of it being ripped away from him made him anxious. How soon could he get Sarah to the altar?

20

B randon propped himself up on his elbow and looked down on Sarah. "What's that beautiful smile for?" he asked. The gnats had decreased since they'd arrived — at least, it sounded like they had.

"I'm happy." Sarah reached her hand up, resting her palm on Brandon's cheek. It pleased her that Brandon had purchased a pair of trimming scissors. She couldn't imagine how long his facial hair would have been after letting it grow the length of time they'd been on the mission. She didn't care, though, knowing she'd find him irresistible regardless of how much or how little facial hair he had. Right now, it felt perfect underneath her fingertips. "Dahabo and Adolphe will marry this weekend and raise their baby when he or she is born."

"It was awesome of Lily to go back to work tonight. Dahabo seemed like a new person after the IV." Brandon said as he rested his arm on Sarah's hip. "Knowing that Dahabo will get the appropriate medical care makes leaving easier. I am going to miss these kids, though."

"That's my girl." Sarah had always been proud of Lily. "I am going to miss them when they go to Haiti and then wherever after that. I wonder if they will ever settle down and have kids of their own?"

Brandon's voice lowered, "You and Jake did an amazing job raising her. She and Kurt are both smart kids. They'll make great decisions."

Sarah thought hearing Jake's name would set her back, but it didn't. Ever since their boat ride with the crocodiles (that's how she referred to her day out with Brandon), she'd embraced the fact that Jake would always be part of her life and not let him come between her relationship with Brandon. "Thank you. We tried our best, for sure."

Popping up on her elbow to bring her face closer to Brandon's, Sarah took a deep breath. "As miserable as it has been without you, everything happens for a reason. I allowed my heart to make room for you. Thank you for being able to share space with Jake." Sarah paused. "I want you to know that I love you, not more or less than Jake, just differently."

Brandon captured Sarah's lips. His free hand traveled up her back and rested on her neck, allowing his fingers to weave through her hair. Instead of kissing her with a heat of passion, it was tender and slow. With every brush of his lips, he made her feel loved, honored and cared for. "Thank you for standing up for me," Sarah spoke against his lips before reconnecting.

Pulling back, Brandon gently combed her hair with his fingers and tucked a tendril behind her ear. "I am honored to share your heart. I've waited so long for you to say that. I love you, Sarah." His hands cupped her face; he tilted it slightly, then deepened the kiss. They matched kiss for kiss before he rested his forehead on hers. "I will always stand up for you. I wanted to knock his teeth out. I won't let anyone disrespect you."

He didn't give her a chance to respond to his sentiment. His lips confiscated hers, not that she was complaining. He tasted like coconut. Her hands smoothed over his impressive shoulders while his hands roamed her entire back before clenching onto her waist. Sarah let a sigh escape when he pulled her impossibly closer to him. With a heaving chest, Brandon pulled back somewhat and gazed into her eyes, "I am so in love with you," he said before gently pressing his lips to hers.

"Sarah?" Trepidation filled his voice.

"Oh no. Your tone doesn't sound good." Her light chuckle made him smile.

"This might seem silly, but I've been wondering..." Brandon paused long enough that she thought he wouldn't finish, but he did. "Are you okay with me going to Florida with you?"

"Is that where Lily and Kurt have us going?" Sarah wondered aloud since she hadn't even looked at the itinerary on her ticket.

"Yes." He gently pushed her shoulder. "Were you just going to show up at the airport and wait for them to tell you where you were going?"

"When you say it like that, it makes me sound like a flake. In reality, I trust my daughter." She shoved his shoulder back, but he didn't move. "Yup, you're like a concrete wall — unmovable."

Brandon's thunderous laugh filled the tent. "Sarah, three days after we arrive in Florida, we're scheduled for a flight to Maine. Drill Sergeant Lily thinks we can get you packed up and moved in three days." He searched her eyes. "Are you sure you want to move back to Maine?"

"She's not wrong. I barely unpacked anything." Sarah admitted, embarrassed.

Brandon's voice piqued, "You still have unopened boxes from five years ago?" He pulled her in for a hug. "That's definitely not the Sarah I know."

Sarah ran her arms up his back. "I am ready to move back, marry you, and grow old with you." She leaned back a little and kissed the pulse point on his neck. He let out a low growl before he wrapped his arms around her waist, pulling her onto his side so her leg draped over one of his.

He winked at her. "Sarah Morris, you are the most beautiful woman in the world. Thank you for allowing me to show you how special you are."

She ran her finger through his hair and scoffed, "I think you have that backward. Thank *you* for giving me a second chance. I will show you how much you mean to me every single day of our lives."

Brandon grinned at her and then devoured her lips. Goosebumps permeated her arms as he weaved his hands through her hair. Their make-out session was cut short when his breath hitched.

"I've missed you, but we're going to do this right." Sarah smiled at Brandon as he let out a long, slow breath. "We need to stop right now. Mark my words, Woman, we will be married the first weekend we're back in Maine." Sarah tilted her head back, letting out a boisterous laugh.

"You think that's funny?" Brandon asked, and then he started tickling her. She rolled off his side in the fetal position, trying to block his hands, but his hands were too big to stop.

"Stop, please." When he finally pulled back, Sarah inhaled deeply. Moving to a seated position, she rested her elbows on her knees. "I can't believe we're leaving the day after tomorrow. I'm excited to see Victoria Falls with Lily and Kurt, but I'm sad we aren't climbing Mount Kilimanjaro."

Brandon rested his palm on her back. "I'll do whatever you want. We can change the tickets around so we can climb and leave from here instead, or we can keep our plans with Lily and Kurt."

Sleep escaped Sarah. She heard the gnats buzzing, though not as bad as the last few weeks. The noise, which annoyed her when she first arrived, reminded her of a peaceful white noise now. Her heart twitterpated all night as she thought about how willing Brandon was to change plans to make her happy. She couldn't believe that her body had finally found that emotion again. In a matter of weeks, her gloomy, depressed state changed into joy just being in Brandon's presence. *Lord, please don't let me mess this up.*

As the country approached its dry season, Sarah found sleeping in the warm weather more difficult. Even without a shirt, Brandon's body radiated enough heat to keep her warm, too, so she ripped off her sweatshirt at some point during the night.

By the time Brandon woke up, the tent felt like a sauna inside. Natives had told her they anticipated an extra dry season this year, which meant it would be even hotter than usual. Apparently, their change in season was a week or two earlier than expected.

"Morning, Beautiful." Brandon stretched out his hand, tracing her back.

"Hey," her voice soft as she leaned back on her pillow, "I couldn't sleep early this morning, so I called my dad for five minutes. I can only imagine how much that will cost." Sarah waved her hand and took a deep breath. "Anyway, I can't wait to see my dad and Barbara. He already knew about us going to Florida first."

"Imagine that," Brandon smirked. "Are you ready to take down what has been our home for the last couple of weeks?"

The sad thought washed over Sarah. It'd been a whirlwind: watching Lily and Kurt get married, agreeing to this mission trip, reuniting with Brandon, becoming his fiance again, and helping Dahabo and Adolphe's families unite. She was going to miss them. Africa might be her new favorite place on earth.

"Are you okay, Love?" Brandon stopped rolling up the sleeping bags when he noticed Sarah lost in her thoughts.

"I'll be good." He wrapped his arms around her waist, pulling her close. She rested her head on his chest. "I hope Adolphe and Dahabo are safe, have a good marriage, and raise a wonderful family."

"Is that all? You're not asking for too much." He chuckled, earning him a playful swat on the arm. "Seriously, you are the best woman I've ever known." He brushed his lips against her forehead and trailed more kisses down her cheek. "Thank you for giving us another chance."

"Thank you." Sarah pressed on her toes while simultaneously pulling him toward her. Their lips met in a gentle game of Twister. For some reason, kissing Brandon felt different this time. She felt how much he loved her, but she also felt the adoration she had for him. Without a doubt, she was meant to reunite with Brandon. In a few short weeks, she'd be his wife.

Brandon ran his knuckle down her cheek. "I hate that we've missed out on the last five years with each other, but I know everything happens in God's timing. I feel a difference in the way you kiss me – you've given yourself to me completely. I am madly, deeply in love with you."

Sarah could feel it, too, like they were truly connected and ready to start their lives together. The emotions Sarah had experienced revolving around her relationship with Brandon were enough to give her whiplash. First, the initial giddiness when she first met him led to guilt when she developed strong feelings for him. Then, she convinced herself that she would upset Jake if she moved on with her life. Like a fool, she walked away, leaving her depressed and withdrawn. Thankfully, Lily tricked them into a mission trip where she and Brandon could reunite. Now, her entire being radiated like the sun, sharing her love with Brandon.

"Dad wants you to know he expects you to 'seal the deal' this time." Sarah shook her head when Brandon's belly laugh shook them. "He also said that Barbara, Pastor Pete, Pearle, and Miss Clancy will be welcoming us home with dinner next Friday."

"Awesome," Brandon smirked, breaking free from their hold to start tearing down the tent to avoid letting her see his face. "That means we're sticking with our plans to visit Victoria Falls."

Sarah cocked her head to the side. "That grin tells me you're up to something."

"Leave him alone, Mom." Lily and Kurt strolled up behind them.

Sarah laughed. "Now I know you're up to something. I never thought my daughter would be a traitor."

Lily sidled up to Kurt and wrapped her arms around his waist. "Everything I've done, it's been for you and your happiness," Lily explained.

"What?" Sarah whipped her hands to her hip. "You're acting like you're the mom." Sarah moved toward her daughter. "I really appreciate your thoughtfulness," Sarah whispered as she hugged her daughter fiercely.

"I don't want to break this up, but if we're going to catch our flight, we need to move." Brandon gestured to the tent. "Many hands make light work."

Sarah loved Brandon with every ounce of her being. Sarah would always be there to help him for as long as she lived.

21

T he next day, the two couples were up at dawn despite enjoying a sunset cruise the night before. They only had one full day to enjoy the scenery. To their dismay, they couldn't fit all the adventures in without rushing from one to the next. They had some decisions to make.

This morning, Lily and Sarah's shriek from the balcony had Brandon rolling off the twin-sized bed. He wouldn't complain that he couldn't stretch out because the footboard was about two feet too short. He wasn't sure what was worse, the elf-sized bed or the hard ground for the last three weeks.

"What is wrong?" Kurt beat Brandon to the women — he chalked it up to the age difference and his horrible sleeping arrangement. The younger man had a queen-sized bed he was sharing with his wife. *Life can be very unfair. Settle down; your time will come.*

Lily pointed at the watering hole. "Look at that giraffe. It's doing a split, well, basically, to get water. That's so cute."

Kurt wrapped his arms around his wife from behind and nuzzled his nose in her neck. Brandon felt a pang of jealousy. Then he reminded himself that he'd soon be a newlywed.

"The man who checked us in yesterday told me that he saw an elephant at the watering hole yesterday, and last week, a lion scared off a buffalo.

Can you imagine watching that in person?" Lily's thrilling voice was contagious.

"Let's get going." The excitement in Sarah's voice and her fingertips on Brandon's forearm warmed his heart. Lily may have made the arrangements for these accommodations but did so at his request. Sarah mentioned wanting to see animals from her room, so here they are, watching animals gather their morning water. Making sure he made Sarah happy was Brandon's top priority in life. For today, he hoped he picked the right excursions, not wanting Sarah to be disappointed.

He pressed a soft kiss to her cheek. "Your wish is my command. Let's go."

She giggled as she grabbed his hand and tugged him back into the room to get ready.

Being in Africa was surreal enough for Brandon, but now after being in Tanzania, he appreciated the differences between there and Zimbabwe. They were in a town in southern Africa in Tanzania surrounded by villages and people, whereas the wilderness surrounded them here in Zimbabwe. It confused him how Sarah could be so afraid of crocodiles yet want to stay somewhere where equally dangerous wildlife — elephants, buffalo, lions, and vultures — resided. He would never understand her thinking.

Walking was one similarity between the two countries, which he also welcomed. Brandon hadn't worked out since he left Maine. Yeah, he'd played sports with the boys, went on the guided run of Mount Kilimanjaro with Kyle, and walked everywhere, but maybe he could get in one workout at the fitness center before they left here.

Watching Sarah's reactions to the wilderness during their two-and-a-half-mile walk from their lodging to the falls made Brandon's heart skip a beat. "Oh, Brandon, look at the elephants over there?" she said, grabbing his arm and bringing him to a halt. Even after all this time, her touch sent sparks cascading down his limbs. A renegade thought put a smirk on his face.

"What are you thinking?" Sarah questioned. Brandon cupped her elbow, pulling her to his chest. His other hand wrapped around her waist. "So far, I like your thinking, Mr. Taylor."

Brandon leaned his cheek into hers, whispering his fantasy. "I was thinking about backing you up to that wall and kissing you until morning."

The quiet shriek that Sarah produced made him chuckle. Her fake reprimanding fell short when she fisted the front of his shirt and pulled him closer as she reached for his lips. He wouldn't deny the woman anything she wanted, especially when it involved kissing.

"If we finish early enough, we could go on an elephant ride," Brandon suggested against her mouth.

Sarah shook her head, creating space between them, as Lily and Kurt joined them. "Nah. If we had time for anything, I'd choose bungee jumping off the Victoria Falls Bridge."

Kurt scoffed. "Are you serious?" He pointed toward the strip connecting Zimbabwe and Zambia.

"She's not," Lily assured him. "It was my mistake to mention it."

"You put the idea in her head?" Kurt questioned, aghast.

Lily shrugged her shoulders, not sure what to say.

Sarah moved toward Kurt, who was looking a little green in the face. "Don't pass out on us; there probably isn't enough time for both."

"Clearly, Kurt doesn't want to bungee jump. What about an elephant ride?" Brandon suggested.

The newlyweds shook their heads in agreement. Brandon's gaze shifted to Sarah. "Are you willing to give up your bungee jumping, or at least put it on hold so your son-in-law doesn't have a heart attack on us?"

Sarah mimicked the thinking emoji with her pointer resting over her pursed lips, head, and eyes tilted up toward the sky. " I guess so. If it keeps this man around for my daughter a little bit longer, I can sacrifice the fun."

"Pshaw! I just kept you around a little longer for this man. Have you seen the death rate for bungee jumping?"

Sarah shook her head. "Nope. if it's my time to go, I'll go, whether I'm bungee jumping or walking on the street. I'd rather go having fun than getting hit by a bus or something."

"You really mean that, don't you?" The corner of Kurt's lips lifted, and he let out a little puff of breath. "I'm amazed at people's ability to think like that."

"Alright, let's go!" Brandon urged. They started walking again. "I'm glad Lily planned this. You have all the secrets of visiting here." Brandon complimented the girl, who was like a daughter to him.

"I might be able to go bungee jumping," Kurt stated, unable to let that conversation end; trepidation filled his voice.

The rest of the group laughed but quickly stifled it, and all was forgotten when they reached the falls. They stared silently at the falls for seconds, minutes, or hours — Brandon couldn't ascertain. Sarah put her hand to her heart. "This is..."

"Breathtaking," Brandon murmured in her hair. The spray from one of the seven wonders of the world soaked them.

He wrapped his arms around Sarah's shoulders. They stood like that longer than he expected, but it brought him such peace. He was staring at one of the world's seven wonders, holding the most beautiful woman in the world.

Sarah leaned her head into Brandon's bicep. "We can go whenever you're ready. I could stay here all day." She traced her fingers up and down the length of his arm.

"I don't know if there's much point in walking to the Zambia side since it's all dried up, but we could swim in Devil's Pool," Brandon suggested. Sarah's look of appreciation filled his chest with pride. All he did was Google different activities to do when visiting Victoria Falls, but Sarah gave him a look like he hung the moon.

Visiting Victoria Falls during the hottest month of the year didn't seem like a great idea now that the heat smothered him. If he put some space between him and Sarah, he might not sweat so much, but that wasn't about to happen. If she didn't complain, he certainly wouldn't. She already knew that he sweat, even in the middle of the cold Maine winters, and she still loved him.

Lord, please help me appreciate your beautiful masterpiece in front of me — this time, I'm not talking about Sarah. Brandon wanted, more than anything, to get home and marry this beautiful woman. He needed to be content with where he was right now — facing one of the world's seven wonders. *I'm sorry, Lord, for my lack of focus. Help me enjoy this opportunity you've given me.*

"Hey, we're going to swim in Devil's Pool," Lily informed her mom and Brandon.

Sarah stepped forward, placing a gap between her and Brandon. "So are we. Let's go." She laced her fingers with Brandon's and tugged him along.

Swimming dangerously close to the edge of the fall, Sarah and Lily asked Kurt to take their picture.

"You ladies are crazy." Kurt snapped the picture. "You know that like a hundred-foot drop, right?"

"I don't plan on going over, so I think I'm good." Sarah countered.

Brandon shook his head. "Real comical. Now that you've got your picture, can you swim back this way?"

"You, too, please." Kurt requested his wife to move away from the edge.

Both women looked at each other. Brandon wondered what they were thinking. Knowing both of them, they were contemplating whether or not to give a smart-alec response. Instead, they just moved back to the depth of the pool.

Brandon opened his arms to Sarah, who snuggled up against his side, molding perfectly to his side. "When we get home, I'd like to build a deck with a hot tub for us to enjoy," he said.

"Really?" Sarah's eyes looked adoringly at Brandon. "That sounds wonderful." Resting her head on his chest again. "We haven't talked about what our future will look like. Are we going to live at your place?"

"Do you want to live at my place and make it ours, or should we build our own?" Brandon's voice was tender and sincere.

"I'm not sure. I do like your house. What would you like to do?"

He kissed the top of her head. "I'll do anything you want, Sweetheart." Her cheeks turned light pink. He loved seeing her blush, knowing he made it happen. Brandon really didn't care. He'd heard of men just giving in and letting their wives make those types of decisions, or they'd never hear the end of their nagging. Brandon was lucky that Sarah didn't nag, but that's not why he let her choose. It brought him pure joy to see her happy. Knowing he made her happy was the whipped cream on top of his milkshake.

"Maybe we can decide that once we arrive home," Sarah suggested.

"Anything you say, Love," Brandon whispered against her cheek before he placed a warm kiss on her cheekbone.

As a newlywed couple, they would make a lot of decisions. Brandon thought it would be nice to stay in his house, but he'd build her a mansion if she wanted it. Thankfully, he knew her well enough to know that she didn't care about showy items. His log cabin would be fantastic for her, and he loved that about her. She may want to add some femininity to the place, and he couldn't wait for flowery throw pillows, scented candles, or whatever girly things she wanted to introduce into their home.

After a long, relaxing soak in The Devil's Pool, the sun began to dip below the horizon, bidding farewell to their last day in Africa. In its wake, red, orange, and gold hues stained the sky. Both couples changed before they trekked back to the lodge for dinner.

The authentic dinner and drum show didn't disappoint. Upon arriving, Sarah and Lily received a dot painted on their face — to represent the beauty of African women. Brandon and Kurt got lines painted on their faces representing the warrior look of the African men.

"Do you smell that?" Brandon stopped and inhaled deeply. He didn't know what the smell was, but it smelt divine.

"Look at all these authentic meats," Kurt said, rubbing his hands together. Brandon decided to try everything, knowing he'd likely never return to Africa again. The smoked crocodile tail was a delicacy he hadn't expected to enjoy.

Sarah's peppered impala wasn't as welcoming as his, but the intimacy of sharing food off each other's plate made up for the lousy aftertaste from her selection.

"Here, try this peanut butter rice." Sarah scooped some of the carbs on her fork and brought it to my mouth.

"It's not bad. Have you tried it yet?" Brandon asked, looking for her opinion.

Sarah tried a forkful. "Hmmm. This is delicious." Her exaggerated showing had Brandon quirking an eyebrow.

"I don't think it was that good, but I'm glad you like it." Brandon rested his hand on her thigh and gently rubbed his palm up and down its length.

Leaning closer to Brandon, Sarah pressed her lips to his, lingering longer than expected at the dinner table, but Brandon wasn't complaining. As it turned out, the peanut butter rice tasted better on her lips than on the fork.

They needed to leave the lodge by eight in the morning, so they quickly ate dessert and retreated to their rooms to pack.

"I am so happy Lily talked me into coming on this mission trip. Not only did I get to meet Adolphe and the other boys, but God brought you back into my life." Brandon wrapped his arms around Sarah's waist as she leaned over her suitcase, folding and organizing her clothes. He pulled her upright, sniffing her shampoo — the coconut fragrance made him want to sit on the beach with her.

Sarah turned to face him. "Mr. Taylor, this has been the best trip of my life." She kissed his cheek.

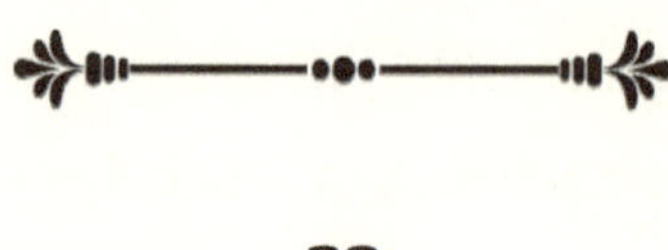

22

Large snowflakes fell rapidly from the sky. For the third day in a row, a gray sky loomed over Brookwater, Maine. But Sarah's heart was filled with bright sunshine. She sat on the porch swing, bundled in her thick winter jacket, mittens, and a blanket wrapped over her lap, waiting for Brandon to arrive.

Her dad and Barbara had a combined an engagement and welcome home party for the two couples. Fortunately, Lily and Kurt agreed to stay in Maine for the next month to spend the holidays with the family before heading to their next mission trip in Haiti.

Headlights shone in the driveway. Sarah had expected it to be Brandon. Instead, Miss Clancy pushed open the driver's side door. She tried to pull herself up using the door handle but couldn't. Sarah bounded down the front steps and rushed to help her. Sarah loved Miss Clancy, partly because she was Marlene, Sarah's late mom's best friend, and because she had an angel's heart. She truly cared about others and put them before herself.

Sarah preoccupied herself by catching up with Miss Clancy and learning more about her new friend, Bill. After graduating college, Bill inherited his father's well-established shipping business. Already a billionaire, the silver-haired man decided to retire and leave the business in his well-trained daughter's hands back home in Texas. He had more money than he knew what to do with, so he returned to Maine, where he'd left a beautiful twenty-year-old almost forty years earlier.

Before their senior year of college, Bill met Miss Clancy at the local Camp Sunshine. She worked for the camp yearly and loved seeing the children smile. His father forced him to work there under an alias to show his son how the rest of the world lived. It only took that summer for the two of them to fall in love, but when the camp closed for the season and Bill boarded his plane, they promised to write and stay in touch.

Sadly, the distance proved to be too much. Neither ever wrote, hoping the other would write first. Within a few years, both married other people, but they always remembered that summer. Both experienced wonderful marriages that ended too soon, numerically speaking. They relished in pure joy with the birth of their children; his wife gave him a girl, and Miss Clancy gave her husband two sons. While they loved their spouses, they never forgot one another. They were both single again and retired and enjoying their lives together.

Sarah's memory returned to the day she called off the wedding. Miss Clancy sandwiched her hands around Sarah's. "Dear, only God knows what is right. That said, you best be praying because this feels all wrong to me. I don't want you waking up one day regretting this decision."

Miss Clancy had had her back every day since, but she didn't miss an opportunity to tell Sarah she'd made a big mistake letting 'that hunk of a man' go. Thankfully, Brandon had forgiven her, and they were preparing for their wedding.

When Miss Clancy found out that Sarah and Brandon were engaged again, her dad told her that Miss Clancy shrieked louder than Sarah and Gus put together.

"Are you okay, Miss Clancy?" Sarah reached for the older woman's elbow and guided her to her feet.

"Ever since that surgery, I've been miserable. God's got this, though. How are you, my dear?" Embracing Miss Clancy was heavenly, just like hugging her mom. It'd been years since she'd seen Miss Clancy — she looked thin and feeble, causing Sarah's heart to cry.

At that moment, Brandon pulled in and quickly hopped out of his truck. "Miss Clancy, how are you doing this fine day?"

"Same, handsome." Sarah noticed the tinge of pink on Brandon's cheeks, which she found highly endearing and attractive.

"Morning, Sweetheart." Brandon kissed Sarah on the cheek. "I can take over from here. It's our thing." Sarah backed away as Brandon stepped toward Miss Clancy, who tried to protest but shrieked instead. Brandon swooped her into his arms and carried her into the house. "This is a much faster ride, eh?"

Miss Clancy's high-pitched voice made Sarah laugh. "You don't need to carry an old woman like me around. You should be carrying Sarah around."

"But she can walk just fine. Why would I do that?" Brandon winked at Sarah, who had caught up with them, and rushed ahead to open the door.

After getting Miss Clancy settled, Brandon found Sarah admiring the Christmas tree that her dad and Barbara had set up earlier that morning. He wrapped his arms around her waist and nestled his nose in her neck. "I'd carry you anywhere. You know that, right?"

Sarah giggled. "Sure do." She wrapped her arms around his neck. "Don't dismiss the appeal you draw, helping Miss Clancy out like that."

"You found that sexy, didn't you?" Brandon turned Sarah around, and their gaze met. Brandon leaned in without taking his eyes off her, but her strong palm on his chest stopped him.

Sarah stepped out of his space and shrugged to prevent his ego from getting out of control. "I plead the fifth." They walked, hand-in-hand, through the spacious living room into the dining room, where Barbara had everything perfectly set. The welcome home feast consisted of their traditional Thanksgiving dinner since Kurt and Lily were heading to Haiti for another three-week-long mission, missing the American holiday. They'd be home the third week in December through the end of the year.

In addition to turkey, mashed potatoes, butternut squash, sweet potato casserole, and green beans, dinner consisted of Sarah's favorite, lasagna, and Brandon's favorite, angel hair with bolognese sauce.

Brandon's actions kindled her affection for him. His doting on Miss Clancy assured her he'd be gentle with her as they aged together. When he rested his hand on Sarah's thigh under the table as Gus pressed her for wedding details, she knew he'd support her through life's ups and downs.

"Please tell me you two have set a date not too far away." Gus shoveled a fork full of lasagna into his mouth.

"We are going to get through the holidays first, Gus, then we'll get married," Brandon winked at Sarah.

Gus scoffed. "That didn't work out so well last time. Are you sure that's a good plan?" Her dad, never at a loss for words, always said what he thought, even if it didn't sound right in his out loud voice.

She grinned at her dad. "We'll have to discuss it and let you know." Brandon pinned his eyes on her, probably wondering what she was thinking. How he looked at her... talked to her...doted on her... Sarah wasn't sure she could wait until after the holidays to marry this man.

Dinner lasted another hour. Sarah was genuinely shocked when Miss Clancy ate nothing. "Exactly what happened during your surgery?" Sarah asked, clasping her fingers together and resting her hands on the table.

"I've told you everything over the years. Seeing me in person and what life is like daily is very different from what it sounds like on paper." Guilt pierced Sarah's heart. Had she been so caught up in her drama that she only heard what poor Miss Clancy had been through and not listened? Imagine a doctor messing up that much on a stomach surgery and leaving the patient to suffer.

Meanwhile, she'd been down in Florida doing nothing. . .productive. She could have taught from Maine, and she and Brandon may have already reconciled before now, and she would have been here for her mom's best friend. *Lord, please forgive me for being so selfish. Thank you for watching out for Miss Clancy. Please take her out of this pain. You can heal her with the snap of your fingers. Make the doctor fix this. She's a wonderful lady and doesn't deserve this.*

"I'm so sorry I wasn't here for you — for all of you." Sarah's throat was clogged with emotion.

Sarah winced when Brandon said, "We forgive you. Everything happens for a reason." His palm gliding along her back calmed her. Miss Clancy shook her head in agreement.

How could he be so understanding? He bared the depths of his soul for everyone at the table to see. Okay, so. This man was an angel sent from heaven above, and she would make sure he knew he was one of the most influential people — *top three, counting her dad and Lily* — in her life.

"I think we should get married before Christmas," Sarah blurted out on the truck ride to Brandon's house, which would soon be hers, too. Brandon's shocked look answered her question of whether or not she'd been too dramatic in her outburst.

"That came out of nowhere." Brandon chuckled and returned his eyes to the road.

Sarah composed herself. It'd been a perfect dinner with her family, and now she wanted an ideal evening with Brandon. Light snow had started to fall, leaving unique speckles on the windshield. As much as Sarah loved her Florida heat, the romantic feelings sparked by a gentle snowfall made her feel all warm and gooey inside. Going home, sitting by the fire, and leaning against Brandon's chest sounded like the most incredible ending to an already fantastic day.

Since reuniting with Brandon, she'd been waiting for the best time to discuss this. "Not really. At least not to me — I've been thinking about this for a little while now. I just didn't say anything ." Sarah sighed; this conversation needed to happen. "I spent the last five years being mad at myself for letting the devil convince me that I was doing the wrong thing by marrying you. I don't want to waste another minute apart."

Brandon parked his truck in the garage and killed the engine. Sarah released her seatbelt and slid toward him, her knee pressing against his thigh. "Ever since you stepped on that plane, I knew God had given us a second chance. I am ready to call you my husband. No, I am more than ready. I want nothing else than to call you my husband. I'd marry you tomorrow if you wanted."

"You are dangerously beautiful," Brandon whispered.

His voice was full of raw emotion that pierced Sarah's heart. She dipped her head toward the floor. "Have you decided where you want to live?"

Brandon placed his forefinger under her chin and lifted it gently until their eyes met. "Wherever you are is where I want to be." Brandon opened his mouth, but Sarah cut him off. "I won't object if you want to live in a warmer climate." She winked at him.

Brandon placed his hands on her shoulders. "You may have to prepare yourself for what I'm about to say." He leaned closer, almost touching her cheek. "I don't want to move you away from here. I wouldn't miss my opportunity to keep you warm all winter." He winked at her before he pressed his lips on hers. At first, his mouth moved slowly, even tenderly, over Sarah's, melting into her. He finished his thought against her lips, "But if you want to move away, I'll be the first to pack." Then, he cupped the back of her neck and weaved his hand through her thick hair as he titled his head one way, hers the other. She pulled at the sides of his open flannel shirt to get him closer. Albeit, any closer, and she'd be on his lap.

They pulled apart, their breathing shallow, chests heaving, and if his thoughts were anything like hers, Sarah wanted more – *more kissing, more touching, more smoldering looks, more Brandon.*

23

"I never knew it was possible to sweat that much in the winter." Gus cackled at his soon-to-be son-in-law.

Brandon forced a smile, unsure if it reached his face. "Besides the fact that I always run hot, this is nerve-racking."

"According to Lily, she's here and ready to go, so relax." Kyle chuckled as he slapped Brandon on the shoulder.

The pastor and his wife, Gus and Barbara, and Brandon's parents spent all day yesterday decorating the sanctuary for the ceremony and Fellowship Hall for the reception. The burnt orange, maroon, and golden flowers on the ends of the aisles and around an archway where the ceremony will take place, along with centerpieces, expressed the season perfectly. "It looks like firecrackers in here," Brandon said aloud as he gently rubbed the orange rose petals between his thumb and forefinger.

"Yes, it's bright in here." Brandon turned at the sound of Pastor Pete's voice. "I guess you made the right decision to go on the mission trip."

"I sure did." Brandon extended his hand, which the pastor clasped onto and pulled Brandon in for a one-armed, manly hug.

Brandon was dressed to the nines in a traditional black tux with a white carnation pinned to his lapel, and he finally stopped his nervous pace. The ceremony – his wedding – would start soon.

His parents sat front and center for the small ceremony. He watched his dad pass his mom a tissue. She was already crying! *Goodness, Mom, wait for the ceremony to start.* Brandon chuckled inwardly.

"You look so handsome." Evelyn placed her palm on Brandon's cheek and wiped her eyes with the tissue in her other hand.

"Thanks, Mom." Brandon kissed her cheek.

"Do you have the rings?"

Brandon tapped his leg right about the pocket. "Right here."

"I'm going to mingle before the ceremony starts." She kissed her son on the cheek.

Caleb Taylor had spent his son's adult life trying to convince him to build his construction business. Much to his chagrin, Brandon refused every time, causing Caleb to argue with his son. By the grace of God, Caleb had given up on pressuring Brandon to expand.

"I'm proud of you, Son." Caleb slapped one hand on his son's shoulder and extended the other. "I'm sorry for all the years we argued over what you should do with your business, and it looks like you knew what you were doing all along."

Wow! Dad never admits when he's wrong. "Thanks, Dad, I appreciate that."

"When are you leaving?" Caleb asked.

Brandon rubbed his palms together quickly. "Right after the ceremony, we're heading to Bermuda for the honeymoon, and then we'll join the kids in Haiti."

"I never thought you could be happy only working part of the year and being a missionary the rest of the year. You are an amazing man, making a difference in the world."

This dad's words touched Brandon's heart. He pulled his dad's shoulders toward him and embraced him like never before.

"Thanks for helping me get ready today," Sarah said in a shaky voice, glancing at her daughter in the mirror while fixing the back of her dress.

"You are beautiful." Miss Clancy chimed. "Your mother would be so proud of you. Thank you for letting me fill in for her today."

Everyone's emotions were high today. Not only was this wedding five years past due, but Sarah's mom was only with them in spirit. She'd already cried a pool of tears for her mother this morning. Lily had to work extra hard to eliminate the puffy redness.

"Thank you." Sarah turned around to face her daughter, Miss Clancy, and Barbara. "All of you have dropped everything to make this day happen so we could join Lily and Kurt—"

"—Don't forget the honeymoon. You'll be on an island with that hottie of a husband. Now that you guys are married, you make God proud and follow his Word. You may be too old to procreate, but pretend like you can."

"Miss Clancy!" Sarah's voice raised an octave, as did the redness in her cheeks.

"You are one feisty woman." Sarah loved the wisdom Miss Clancy shared whether you asked for it or not.

Barbara cleared her throat. "The people of Haiti will live more comfortably once you and Brandon help build their homes and schools," she said proudly, her voice filling the room.

Sarah chuckled. "It will be interesting to see how well Brandon and I can work on a project together. Not all married people can complete such undertakings together."

"No, they can't, but I don't think you two will have any problems." Miss Clancy winked at Sarah.

Pearle Knight, Pastor Pete's wife, knocked on the door. In unison, all three ladies hollered, "Come in."

"Oh, my." Her hand flew to her mouth. "You are gorgeous."

"Thank you." Sarah smiled shyly.

"We're ready when you are. I'll have your dad wait right outside." Pearle slowly shut the door.

"You got this, Mom." Lily, Barbara, and Miss Clancy left to find their seats in the sanctuary.

Neither Brandon nor Sarah had bridal party members. They felt it was too close to the holidays to spring a wedding on people, so they did word-of-mouth invitations, and Pastor Pete announced it on the church website.

"Hi, Dad." Sarah stepped into the hall. Her dad's eyes pooled instantly when he saw her.

"You look just like your mother, especially in her dress." Gus reached out his hands. "She'd be so proud of you for listening to your heart and God." He wiped the escaping tear with the back of his hand.

"Thank you for supporting me." Sarah let out a slight chuckle. "You were kind of ... annoying with all of your meddling, but that's what makes you the best dad in the world. I love you."

"I love you too, Honey." Gus squeezed his daughter. . .tight.

Trying to push away from her dad, she said, in a strained voice, "Dad, you're cutting off my air supply."

"Sorry." He kissed her on the cheek and extended his elbow. Sarah looped her hand through his arm.

She picked up her bouquet and secured it in her free hand. She wasn't sure about fall flowers, but the florist promised her they'd look magnificent together. She hadn't lied. The pointy thistle's calm blue tone accentuated the rest of the bunch. It matched perfectly with the orange roses, an item Sarah hadn't even known existed. The florist included a golden rod in the bouquet. All these flowers had precise names, but Sarah was so stressed planning this wedding in three days; she was lucky to have flowers, never knowing the scientific name for them. One of her favorites was these long-stemmed, bright golden spheres. She'd have to remember to take a picture with them and write the florists a thank you note.

The minute they heard The Wedding March, Gus opened the door. Sarah locked eyes with Brandon, waiting at the front of the church. Their eyes never left each other. Her belly dipped; excited nerves were rocking out like it was nineteen eighty.

Brandon blinked rapidly. She knew he was trying to prevent tears from falling. He was the most handsome man alive. Too bad she couldn't control her tears. She couldn't blink fast enough; tears slid gently down her cheeks.

When they reached the front of the church, Gus kissed his daughter's cheek and handed her off to Brandon. "Take care of her, Son."

"I will, Gus. Thank you." Brandon took Sarah's hands.

Her stomach flip-flopped under his intense gaze. He leaned forward so only she could hear, "You are stunning." He kissed her cheek and nodded to Pastor Pete to let him know they were ready.

"I must start by saying how honored I am to officiate today's wedding. I've known Sarah all her life, from pigtails and prom dresses to a beautiful daughter and wedding dresses. I love the heart Sarah has for the Lord. She wouldn't do anything to go against God intentionally. That's why we are here five years later than we expected."

A light chuckle from the audience made her blush. Brandon gently squeezed her hands. There was that support again. He was going to be the best husband ever. He supported and encouraged her decisions. Even when he disagreed with them, he never pushed. Instead, he let God's work be done.

"Are you ready to become man and wife?" Pastor Pete's light-hearted tone rang throughout the sanctuary.

"Definitely!" Brandon's eagerness vibrated throughout, bringing on an even louder laugh from the crowd.

"The couple has asked me to do something different for their vows. You all know me. I'm pretty routine, but this is a great idea. I only wish I thought of it myself." Pastor Pete chuckled at his joke, along with everyone else.

"I'm going to read from First Corinthians chapter thirteen. Then I will ask you a series of questions, and you need to answer 'I do' after each one."

Sarah and Brandon shook their heads in unison.

"Brandon, do you promise to be patient with Sarah?"

"I do." His eyes locked with his future wife's.

"Brandon, do you promise to be kind?"

"I do."

"Brandon, do you promise not to envy or boast?"

"I do." He shrugged his shoulder, all cool-like, getting a smirk from Sarah.

"Brandon, do you promise not to be proud or dishonor Sarah?"

"I do."

"Brandon, do you promise not to be self-seeking or easily angered?"

"I do."

"Brandon, do you promise to keep no record of Sarah's wrongdoings?"

"I do."

"Brandon, do you promise to shun evil and always be truthful?"

"I do."

"And finally, Brandon, do you promise always to protect Sarah, trust her, put your hope in her, and let your love for her persevere right after your relationship with the Lord?"

"I do." Brandon pressed their hands together even tighter.

"Just because I've been married, and I know this one is crucial too. . ." Pastor Pete winked at his wife, sitting in the front row. "Brandon, do you promise to try your best to make her laugh at least once daily?"

"I do."

"Alright, Sarah, it's your turn." Pastor Pete asked the same questions of Sarah. Every time she said, "I do," Brandon pumped his fist in the air, getting Sarah and the audience to laugh.

"Brandon, do you have the rings?" Pastor Pete held his palm up for Brandon to place his ring there while he placed Sarah's on her finger. "You have what you'd like to say?"

"Yes."

"Take it away." Pastor Pete smiled at him.

"Sarah, I give this ring as a sign of my love to you and a visual reminder to keep all those promises." He slid the ring on her left finger, and his smile dropped. Brandon gently gripped her wrist, pointing her fingers down, and the ring fell off in his waiting hand.

A little gasp from the audience grabbed his attention. "Hey, if this had happened five years ago, the ring would have fit perfectly; it's not my fault."

The crowd erupted in laughter. Brandon slid the ring on her middle finger. It fit. "This will have to do for now."

Sarah declared the ring as a token of her love for Brandon and glided it onto his finger. It fit perfectly. They planned on getting him a safer one that he'd wear when working.

"Now, before we get to the part Brandon is dying for, I have one more thing to say."

"Hurry up, Pastor." Brandon chuckled, again making the onlookers laugh.

"You made beautiful promises to each other today, and I believe you mean them. But in the daily grind, we sometimes forget many of those promises. So I give you just one promise to remember that will help you achieve all the others."

The Pastor cleared his throat before he continued. "We must cleave unto the Lord. Regardless of how badly people disappoint you or how upset you get with others, you must remember to follow the Lord because He is the only one who will never disappoint you nor forsake you."

"Amen," Sarah stated firmly.

"Alright. By the power vested in me by the State of Maine, I now pronounce you husband and wife. Brandon, you may kiss your bride."

Brandon wagged his eyebrows at Sarah as he pulled her close, putting one arm around her waist. He hoisted her up so she was at his eye level. He said in a deep, throaty voice, "Hello, Mrs. Taylor."

"Hi," she whispered back. One hand resting on his shoulder and the other on his cheek.

"I've been waiting five, long years to say that." Brandon devoured her lips. The spectators cheered, hooted, and hollered like the sanctuary was fully packed.

Sarah loved kissing Brandon, but something about this one was different. Her current state of euphoria matched her erratically beating heart.

Pulling back, Brandon uttered, "Thank you for becoming my wife. I will do my best to keep every promise I made to you."

"I will, too." Sarah kissed her husband's bottom lip and gently tugged on it.

Brandon's next words were close to her ear and low enough just for her to hear. "Well, Mrs. Taylor, let's get this reception over so we can start our honeymoon. It's time to show me that tattoo."

"With pleasure," Sarah said, blushing. They interlaced hands and proceeded down the aisle.

Pastor Pete announced, "Join me in welcoming the new couple, Mr. and Mrs. Taylor!"

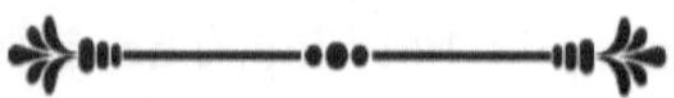

EPILOGUE

January and February are the coldest months in Haiti. That might mean something to the locals who claim it will be so hot in a couple of months they can't breathe. They have thin fabric covering the majority of their arms. To Sarah's husband and the other men from areas prone to frigid temperatures and lots of snow, the high seventies to mid-eighties is summer, shirtless weather.

Despite the breeze from the ocean, hot moisture slid down Sarah's neck underneath her tank top straps as she lugged a two-by-six to Brandon and his crew. "Here you go," Sarah said, using her thigh to hoist the board to her awaiting husband.

He greeted her with a hard kiss on the mouth, making her smile and blush when he pulled back. "Thank you, sweetheart," he said before handing the board to a newcomer.

An unexpected cyclone had produced considerable damage in the northern countryside near the Gulf de la Gonave, taking most the workers from their close-to-the-Caribbean location to fill the needs there, leaving just a skeleton crew until Sarah and Brandon arrived. Lily and Kurt were whisked away instantly to assess and heal those affected by the natural disaster.

Lily guilted Sarah into her first mission trip in October. The idea of spending time with her daughter and son-in-law appealed to her. That's not what happened then, and it isn't what's happening now. Of course, she wanted to still spend time with them, but Sarah genuinely liked the feeling she got when she helped people on these trips.

The number of displaced children hanging around the worksite gnawed at Sarah's organs. They always looked up at Sarah with puppy dog eyes, wanting her to play. In a domino-like fashion, Sarah looked at Brandon in the same way. He always told her to be safe and figured out how to do the job with one less person.

When they decided to extend their time, Sarah almost felt guilty leaving the crew building houses to help the children, but God always provided. Multiple Habitat for Humanity groups arrived, alleviating the workload on those who'd been volunteering for weeks or months by that time. Since arriving, Brandon had built tens homes. Amazing. Now, the crew was working on constructing a school. When they finished, Sarah and Brandon would return home.

Brandon jumped off the two-foot ladder, landing with a light thud in front of his wife. "What's your plan for the day?"

"Marie and Pierre are on their way with some of their friends. I'm taking them to the ocean, and we will work on descriptive writing today," Sarah felt free and light. She loved working with kids of all ages, but this set of eleven-year-old twins gripped her heart the moment they met.

They lost their parents in a hurricane over a year ago. Living with their aunt and uncle, they are forced to work in the fields with their older cousins most days, preventing them from attending school regularly. Sarah's ability to speak French helped break the barrier enough to provide them with fun learning opportunities while they rebuilt.

Brandon draped his arms over Sarah's shoulders while she wrapped her arms around his waist, looping her thumb through the belt loops of his sun-dried jeans. Fortunately, the balmy weather didn't make it unbearable to snuggle with her husband. Her fingertips brushed against a piece of paper protruding from his back pocket. "What's this?" She pulled it out, leaning away from his hold.

"Your dad sent you a thick letter. what do you think it is?" Brandon's curiosity was getting the better of him.

"I don't know. But daylight is burning. Let's finish this, and we can read it together tonight."

"Okay, wifey. I better get back before they go rogue on me." He kissed her forehead and sauntered off. Sarah was unable to look away until the kids tugged on her arm.

"Ready to go?"

They shook their heads and jumped up and down in place.

"Let's go!" They gripped Sarah's hand, one on each side, as they strolled to the beach. Sarah had stopped asking whenever the friends Marie and Pierre invited didn't show. It usually meant they were in the fields. Why did this world have to be so unfair to kids?

The sun bide them farewell for the day. Sarah and Brandon nestled in their single-man tent for the evening. Snuggling with Brandon would never get old. Every night after the final meal, Sarah rested her head in the crook of his arm and drew circles on his chest and abdomen while they shared events of the day. Tonight, Sarah was eager to open the letter from her dad, but Brandon was teasing her with a game of keep-a-way.

Her phone rang, pulling her attention away. "Oh, it's Lily. Pause, please."

"Hi, Honey, how are you?" Her daughter's angelic face beamed through the small screen on her video call. Kurt now joined her to say hi.

"We're good." Lily drew out the vowel sounds in the word *good* a little too long, letting Sarah know she was up to something.

She smiled knowingly at Brandon, but he wasn't sure what she was revealing.

"We have something to tell you unless you want to guess." Lily offered.

"You'll never get it," Kurt challenged.

"Are you sure about that, Son?"

Lily shouted, "We're," while Sarah yelled, "You're," and they both finished with "pregnant!" at the same time. Brandon covered his ears as Sarah's shriek filled the tent.

Once both women stopped their screaming, Brandon congratulated them. "When will we have a little Anderson running around?"

"September, if my calculations are correct," Lily joked like she hadn't previously calculated due dates for thousands of pregnant women.

She knew her daughter would roll her eyes, but the question had to be asked. "What are you planning to do about mission trips and settling down?"

There it was — the Lily Roll — a new name Sarah created for her daughter's chronic eye roll.

"We just told you we were pregnant," Lily stated like that answered the question. It didn't.

Sarah laughed. "That means you've known for at least a week and tried to plan everything out."

"She knows you well, Babe," Kurt kissed his wife's temple.

The Lily Roll didn't disappoint.

"Fine. We plan to settle in Maine if Brandon is willing to build us a house. I will check with Grandpa to see if he will still give us a section of land up back."

All eyes were on Brandon. "Yeah, I'll build you a house."

Another shriek filled the tent. Sarah kissed Brandon's cheek. "The school will be wrapped up in about two or three weeks; then we're heading home. How about you?"

"Our time is up at the end of this week, so we'll meet you back at Grandpa's. I love you guys."

"Love you too," Sarah and Brandon said in unison.

When Sarah hung up her phone, she pressed her palms to Brandon's chest and slid them up around his neck. "I feel too young to be a grandmother, but I'm so excited."

Brandon tightened his arms around Sarah's waist and captured her lips. Many beats later, Brandon trailed kisses along her jaw, whispering to her when he reached her ear. "You'll be the youngest, sexiest grandmother I've ever seen."

Sarah's heart and body shivered under his hands. There was one more thing to take care of before the night got away from them.

"Can we read the letter from my dad and then finish what you're starting?" Sarah asked in a whisper.

Brandon pulled the letter from his back pocket. "Of course."

Sarah ripped it open like a child, expecting money to be hidden inside. Sarah knew that wasn't the case, but she was excited to see what her dad had to say. There were only three pieces of paper, but when they were folded, they seemed thicker.

Dear Sarah and Brandon,					*February 1st*

Barbara and I miss you both. We are counting the days until you arrive home safe and sound. We had a Nor'easter that damaged one of the greenhouses. I've got it patched up until you're home, Brandon. If you'd replace it for me, I'd appreciate that.

Since you decided to stay in Haiti longer, I figured you'd want the letter I included before you arrived home.

It's been a long while since I've seen you and maybe an even longer time since I've said this. I am so proud of both of you. You might have caused me more gray hair in the last few years, but it all worked out. You're spreading the love of God through your volunteering, and you're loving each other. You've made this old man happy.

Love you both, and see you soon!

Dad

Sarah wiped a tear from her eye. "I miss my dad." Brandon wrapped his arms around Sarah and held her while she moved that page behind the others.

Dear Brandon and Miss Sarah –

Dahabo and I are doing fine, and so is the baby. We have a doctor who takes good care of my girls. This doctor has been here since Lily left. She's planning on staying for good. We need her. Dr. Jessie is her name. She seems to know my dad more than they let on. I overheard them talking, and they mentioned your name, Sarah.

I don't pretend to be wise, but I understand. Thank you for making sure our baby and Dahabo got the care they needed. Dahabo's tutor, who also showed up after you left, is helping her progress nicely. My dad has been more at ease and relaxed since you left, too. We no longer have men threatening him and the rest of the family. For that, it seems, I must thank you as well.

You've given my family a second start at life, and Dahabo and me the best start we could have ever asked for. I will never be able to repay you. But I am thankful and wanted you to know.

We are naming our girl Sarah in honor of you. Will you please be her Godparents? Dahabo drew you a picture on the last page.

One last thing: Omri and his whole family died in an attack on their village. Someone said that Omri fought like a champ, but there were too many. He always said he'd rather die than work for any group. Please put all of us on your prayer lists; it's getting worse every day.

We will talk soon.

-Adolphe and Dahabo

A tear fell on the picture Dahabo drew for them. The stick figures with names labeled above them made Sarah smile. Seeing the picture version of her and Adolphe holding hands is just as sweet as the real thing. But the precious baby next to Dahabo's hand, with the name *Sarah* above it, turned her heart to liquid.

"What is Adolphe talking about?" Brandon gently asked.

Sarah shrugged her shoulders. "I didn't need the money I'd saved over the years, so I gave it to Adolphe's dad. That helped him pay off all his debt and have some to keep for next time." Sarah paused, recalling the heartfelt conversation she'd had with Hassan that night the families gathered for dinner. "Lily introduced me to the new doctor. We figured out an amount that would give Dahabo the healthcare she needed. . ." Sarah's words fell short.

Brandon kissed the top of Sarah's head. "You're amazing."

"Grandparents and Godparents, all in a day, what more could we ask for?" Sarah asked, drying her cheeks with the back of her hands.

"Nothing. I have everything I need and want." Brandon wrapped his arms around his wife and pulled her to his chest, closing the gap between them. "I love you, Sarah Taylor."

"I love you too, Brandon Taylor. You've made me complete."

Thank you for reading Sarah and Brandon's second chance love story. They had to travel around the globe to find each other again, but true love can withstand anything.

HOW ABOUT A REVIEW?

Your feedback is valuable, so please consider sharing your thoughts. This will help other readers discover this book and my other works. Thank you from the bottom of my heart for reading and reviewing my book(s).

Amazon
Goodreads
Bookbub

Acknowledgements

"And whatever you do, whether in word or deed, do it all in the name of the Lord Jesus, giving thanks to God the Father through him." ~ Colossians 3:17

Thank you, God, for giving me the opportunity to write and share these stories with the world.

This book is ten years overdue. Thank you to my early readers and supporters of Starting Over, who have asked me many times over the decade, "When is the sequel coming out?" I appreciate you sticking with me, especially you, Kathy B. — everything is in God's time.

I am blessed to have worked with the following people to make Moving On come to life. Thank you to my amazingly supportive family! Without your continued support, this would be a battle.

I have the most astounding BETA readers and ARC team, who dedicated themselves to reading this piece and providing honest feedback and reviews to make my writing better. A special thanks to Laura and Lissa for all your support and suggestions. Thank you for helping promote this piece.

Last but not least, I am grateful for all of you — my readers! Thank you for choosing this story out of the endless options you have. I love writing contemporary romance books, and I hope to provide you with many stories to read soon.

ABOUT THE AUTHOR

Karen Tucci, a public school teacher by profession, now tutors writing students online and homeschools her two children.

A native of Maine, she has trekked miles of the Pine Tree State and visited countless others. It is through her life experiences that the basis for her romance stories develop. One of her favorite things to say when out adventuring is, "...that is definitely going in my next book!"

Fun fact: Karen had only read and wrote non-fiction growing up. It wasn't until her late twenties that she embraced the joy brought forth by doing both — reading and writing — within the different romance tropes. Now she reads at least fifteen fiction novels a month and writes daily!

Connect with Karen:

Facebook Reader's Group.

To find out about special deals, giveaways, and new releases, join her newsletter:

https://www.trueheartromance.com

Instagram

Goodreads

Bookbub

Amazon